To

CW01663563

Race The Undead

When the living fight each other to survive

JONATHAN TRAYNOR

[redacted]

First published in Northern Ireland in 2025 by Excalibur Press

Copyright © Jonathan Traynor

All rights reserved

No part of this publication may be reproduced, stored in a retrieval system, or transmitted, in any form or by any means, electronic, mechanical, photocopying, recording or otherwise without the prior permission of the publisher and copyright holder nor be otherwise distributed in another binding or cover other than that in which it is published.

ISBN
978-1-910728-66-6

Formatting and layout by
Niamh Cooper, Excalibur Press

Cover design by
Andy Pilkington, Very Metal Art

Pic of author by
Lizzie Torbitt

Published by
Excalibur Press
team@excaliburpress.co.uk
excaliburpress.co.uk
07982628911

Dedication

This book is dedicated to my late mother and father and to all the family, even those not bonded by blood.

Acknowledgements

Thanks to Tina and Excalibur Press for all the support, and to Andy Pilkington of Very Metal Art for interpreting my vague brief into a fantastic cover. And to Lizzie Torbitt for tolerating my rants about life in general and this book.

Special thanks to Northern Ireland rock and metal acts *A Little Bitter*, *Conjuring Fate* and *Cursed Sun* for permitting the use of a couple of lines of their songs. Go listen to them on all major streaming platforms or buy their physical copies.

Prologue

The 2020 Covid-19 pandemic was largely controlled by the end of 2024. A combination of vaccination and improved detection, despite the conspiracy theorists and the 'anti-vaxxers', led to a return to what was considered to be normal. Governments had begun to see their debts come under control, albeit with large amounts of austerity. The social media debates on the rights and wrongs of their previous and current actions continued with the usual vitriol. The stock markets went up and down as usual. People complained as much as they always did.

As the world adjusted to the recovery a new threat emerged in Africa and parts of Europe. Scientists at the Defence, Science and Technology Laboratory at Porton Down alerted the UK Government with their concerns. They then began a co-ordination with laboratories across the world. They were astonished when similar worries were expressed, not only by NATO allies, but with Russian, Chinese, Indian and Brazilian contemporaries who surprised all by getting in touch. All pointed, not to a virus, but a combination between a bacterium and an unknown toxin that crossed the blood brain barrier. The results were apparent death. Except the victims were not dead as such. Their brain chemistry was destroyed, except that part of the hypothalamus that controls hunger – they reanimated with a ravenous hunger for flesh from the two 'victims' of this infection they had examined.

As they compared data with their colleagues across the world, they came to the same conclusion, the spread was now too far across the globe to control it.

The Porton Down team agreed that, even with their strict controls, they could not hope to prevent it escaping their facility. A final message was sent to the UK government, then nothing else was heard and attempts to contact them were met with phone silence and all emails were unanswered.

Two days later a special forces squad of eight entered wearing full nuclear, chemical, and biological protection equipment. They found every single scientist, researcher, manager, and member of administrative staff dead. Each shot in the head. The last four of the dead they came across had wounds that were self-inflicted.

In the room where the last four were found was a half-empty bottle of whiskey and a single two-word phrase sprayed in red on a white wall: 'zombie pandemic'.

'Battlesong'

'Some will rise above, some will fall
Some days they beat you down
Some days are better
Raise your hand
Come and join us in a chorus
Of our Battlesong'

A Little Bitter

Part One

SURVIVING

Chapter 1

He stood atop the ancient motte, thinking that more than 900 years ago a Norman knight had stood in this exact spot, one hundred feet above what was street level now and would have been just a rutted path through woods in medieval times.

Had that Norman Knight been defending it from rivals and locals. Was it just a stopping over point before leading further raids? All Greg knew was he wanted to get off it and move.

But he had to wait to hear the engines start and then to light the fuses.

Stretching his long arms, he once more thought that this was just a sci-fi, horror film that was replaying as he dreamt. How many times since his family died, did he have that same thought?

Zombies, evil government agencies and a band of desperate people.

Pulling his webbing tight he swung the rifle from his shoulder. In the distance he heard the engines rev, seemingly tentatively, as if they too were nervous. Looking down at Smicker, he nodded and again wondered how he managed to keep his head shaven amidst the chaos.

A click of the lighter and he began running down the incline thinking how long his 51-year-old body could hold out and his mind stay stable. As he reached Smicker and Seamus they fell in at each side of him and broke into a jog behind the others of the rear guard. Could the 12 of them hold off long enough for the others to reach safety on the coast they talked about often, but never resolved.

Smicker began to ask, 'how big is the explo….' before a massive blast shook the motte, bailey, and the ground beneath their feet.

'What sort of fucking fireworks were you using!' He asked as dirt rained on them, Seamus laughed, and Greg seemed to be about to giggle.

'Let's just say that I found something to give it a boost,' Seamus said.

Those in front of them stood looking up at the blasted hill, needing to be reminded to get moving.

Now they had just to fight their way through the miles, knowing that all but a few had chosen this path because of their health and personal troubled pasts; all knowing that they would not be permitted rescue. The explosion might at least distract some from what they were doing.

They were racing the undead.

Chapter 2

It may have seemed like months since they had received the survivors in Ballymena message from Iceland, but it was just weeks. Huddled around the motte and the meadow in front of it, securing it and the area, never knowing what would happen, just the will to survive driving the first few of those that would gather in this band of survivors.

Tom had brought several radios and transmitters just a few days ago, and after scavenging rechargeable batteries from solar lights in gardens and a rack of other batteries from a shop they had been daily scanning for any signals. Some were ones they had not dared to answer, others were just asking for help. They had assessed which ones to respond to, and which ones to invite to join them when they stumbled on the message.

'This is the Icelandic government, if you are from Ireland or Scotland, please respond. Repeat, if you are from Ireland or Scotland, please respond. This message will be repeated every four hours of the next two weeks only.'

Stunned. Confused. They looked at each other.

'This wee radio won't reach Iceland," said Tom, his broad, ruddy face really alive for the first time since he arrived at the Motte.

'You've an idea Tom," said Greg, noticing the light in his eyes.

'The police station. It has shit in there that could reach the moon,' he said. 'Even some of the better field radios should be enough if we can establish a relay.'

Greg stood, unfolding all 6 foot 2 inches of his lanky frame were seeming to think it over. He pushed his hand through his greying hair.

'Don't you think we've dipped at that well too many

times?'

'Aye, but maybe, just maybe those Icelandic yokes have an idea to help. I mean they did ask specifically about us lot.'

Twice they had been to the station before, guided by Tom. He hadn't been stationed there himself but had been in it many times in his police career. The first visit was to break into the armoury and lift every handgun and semi-automatic rifle there. The second time was to bring ammunition as they had been so nervous in those early days they'd forgotten to get extra rounds.

'Look,' said Tom, 'we get in, grab the radios, and I was meaning to mention this, but we should have looked in the evidence room for extra weapons, so it would be worth the risk to get everybody kitted out.'

Greg looked at the policeman's face reddening as if in anticipation of being outvoted on the idea. Even when excited he thought Tom sometimes talked in clipped tones, as if giving evidence in court. By his own admission, his weight and a shoulder injury had kept him to desk duties, but Greg suspected that once he had been more than just a sergeant on court duties.

'Okay, first light tomorrow, pick three to go with you. Two hours only.'

CHAPTER 3

When Sam, Smicker, Jenny, Rambo, Seamus and their merry band arrived in Ballymena there had just been an intense debate about whether to believe the offer from Iceland.

Not that they arrived without incident, never mind that first few frenetic weeks on the road together. After they picked up the first message, they were directed to Ballymena along back roads, guided past barriers of abandoned cars, told not to walk over certain paths, and as they got to the bottom of the hill a voice simply said "stop".

There were asked pre-arranged questions, gave the pre-arranged answers then told to state the password. Smicker barked it out: 'Bastards!'

One-by-one they walked two steps to the left and as they walked up the hill it was pointed out them a series of booby traps, each with a yellow tape that anyone looking down from the hill could see. Pits with sticks in them, what looked like grenades on wires and a row of tree branches, sharpened, pointing in rows towards anyone coming towards the hill.

'Impressive,' muttered Seamus. Smicker slapped him companionly on the shoulder and began his usual banter and Sam as always blanked their chatter when she needed to concentrate, as the guard gestured up the hill. Standing on the path was a tall man, who introduced himself as Greg as they approached.

As they introduced each other Sam took in what looked like a man of authority, yet with sad, grey eyes.

He had been equally sizing them up. Sam struck him right off as a young woman with an air of ferocity mixed with grace, as they gave him a brief summary of their journey. Her long, blonde hair was tied loosely underneath a baseball cap, blue eyes that seemed to be assessing everything and everybody, and a prominent nose that the rest of her face was shaped around that twitched slightly as she heard anything that seemed interesting.

He cut short his assessment before the rest of their story could be told. 'I'm sure you are all tired. Get something to eat over there, introduce yourself to the others if you wish, and we'll chat more in an hour or so.'

An hour later they found out about the rescue plan.

CHAPTER 4

Tom's hand was shaking as he got ready to press the button to send. They'd jury-rigged a speaker so all could listen. Finally, he pressed send and spoke:

'Icelandic Government, Icelandic Government we are calling from Northern Ireland, please respond.'

A tense three minutes passed before a voice echoed over the speaker.

'Hello, Northern Ireland, good to hear from you. How many of you are there?'

To Greg it seemed a strange question, but before he could voice any concerns Tom responded that there were 75 here and there may be more expected in coming weeks.

The accented voice told them they would contact them in an hour and gave them a new frequency to use.

They muttered a while between them, unwilling to share the news of contact with the wider group just yet, and an hour later they heard a different voice, a woman.

'It is so good to hear from you. We may be able to help you if you are willing. I am Kristin Ólafsdóttir, Prime Minister. Can I speak to whoever can represent the group?'

They all looked at Greg. He theatrically rolled his eyes as he did every time they conferred leadership upon him.

'Good to speak Ms. Ólafsdóttir, I am Gregory, and I have been nominated by my colleagues to speak on their behalf.'

'Please call me Kristin, Gregory. I am going to make this short, for a number of reasons, but I need to ask you a question.

'Can you reach the port of Ballycastle as a group in precisely four weeks?'

Greg paused, feeling the weight of decision heavy, his heart beating worryingly fast.

'May I ask why,' he said.

"If you can, we can bring you to Iceland. We have no outbreaks, we have no real military establishment, but we can defend ourselves, and we need more to do that and establish some sort of future. There are no conditions."

That was the only lie Kristin told them.

Greg said they "probably" could make it to Ballycastle but would need some time to arrange the logistics and promised to speak again in two days.

As he clicked to end the message he just said 'Fuck' not sure he knew whether it was relief, panic or confusion. He looked around the faces. Colin reached him a cigarette as Greg was pulling the, by now, ever-present hip flask from his pocket.

'Well? What do we think?' said Tom. Colin shrugged his shoulders, the rest glanced around the faces.

Greg drew from the cigarette and took a swallow of whiskey, in what he thought must appear to be an over-dramatic gesture but was just him mulling over how to respond.

'I think we should take them up on the offer. We can stay here and get fucked over eventually, or we can take a risk and get the fuck out of here.

'We can only keep ourselves safe for so long and then end up in one last stand like in some shitty movie, or we can take the risk and make the dash for potential safety.'

Colin irritating him by answering: 'Whatever you say boss.' The rest indicated their assent and Greg finished off the rest of the whiskey in the hip flask.

Chapter 5

'Havoc, chaos, and creativity: these are the creeds that we will deliver. These underpin our strategic and tactical ethos. I want each of you to consider what we can do to deceive, disrupt and disorientate whatever we will face when we move out.

'Our Icelandic colleagues will provide some intel on the days that they plan to arrive. By their admission their intel will be at least 12 hours out-of-date. Sam and Smicker, I want you both to co-ordinate the perimeter. Sam, make sure the children are not within 200 metres of the outer perimeter. Smicker, pick people who can at least stay awake.'

'Jenny, when it gets dark, I have a job for you.'

They looked at each other and nodded to Greg as they filed off. He wanted some time to just relax, read and contemplate the many possible ways they could fail and make contingencies, but what he wanted Jenny to do was almost as important as the move in 10 days-time.

'Jenny, if you tell me to fuck off when I ask you to do this job, that's fair enough,' he sighed, lit a cigarette and waited to see if there was any reaction from the women he regarded as the fiercest fighter he had ever encountered but needed to establish herself as someone who could lead.

'We have footage that shows that our perimeter is clear for nearly two miles. What I'm asking you to do comes with some risk, but also plenty of reward to keep morale up.'

'Cut to the chase boss, just what is it you want?'

He smiled, it was that attitude that had led Sam to recommend her so highly to him, no bullshit, no dancing around, just someone who was straight to the point.

'We've ransacked the supermarkets in visual range from the motte, but it was for food but we've not looked for some, shall we say, luxury items.

'I want you to pick 15 people you trust and raid them again but use the river for the nearest two first.

'What is it you want?'

'What I want is to get back without losing anyone or revealing anything to anyone who might be watching. But what I want you really to get is some toys or sweets for the kids and beer, whiskey and cigarettes for us older ones. And coffee would be good too.'

'Are we preparing for war or a party?'

'Fair point,' laughing inwardly but looking straight at her. 'People aren't really that tired, but they are weary, and a little jaded with the waiting around. We won't be moving out for at least 10 days. Everyone is going to be tense. A few, well rationed drinks will help everyone chill out a bit. Besides, I'm nearly out of cigarettes.'

'Fuck you! But on the other hand, it sounds fun...'

He spent the next night sleepless. He knew the probability of Jenny and the team getting into serious trouble was slim, and he had dared not send up any drones lest they give any hints about their position and the forces they had deployed to guard the civilians. Sam and Smicker had questioned his decision until he explained that it was more than getting some 'treats'.

'Jenny has talents, skills and is ferocious, but she needs to learn how to lead people and have people follow her. Whatever you two did in the past leadership comes to you naturally. She hasn't had enough chances. From what you have told me she was content to follow and only step up when in a fight. We need more people who can lead with so many civilians still nervous.'

'You do realise we're civilians too,' muttered Smicker but what Greg said seemed to satisfy them for now, and they retired to check on the night watches without needing to be told.

He now sat at five in the morning sucking desperately on

his last cigarette. Had he asked too much?

The first part of the 'raid' was relatively easy. The man she had chosen as her second in command, John, had managed to build two rafts to navigate the river to their first target. She knew better than to ask how. As it was a balmy night pushing the rafts along in the river, walking them over the weir was easy enough for 16 people. They reached the first supermarket and for the first time she felt the chill of putting people at risk. The multiple exits meant anyone inside could stand a good chance of escaping, but who she sent to patrol the exterior would be vulnerable. As she was about to allocate the tasks, she remembered Ian had been clambering on to trees when she first met him.

"'Ian, do you reckon you can get onto that roof?'

'Sure, easy, peasy, lemon squeezy Jenny.'

With that he took the Barret .50 rifle that Elijah had become possessive of - along with its night scope - and scuttled up a drainpipe like a latter-day Spiderman.

Within minutes two others were patrolling the outskirts and Jenny was pointing out areas for the team to search. She herself headed straight to where she thought would be tobacco and cigarettes. If Greg wanted cigarettes, he was fucking going to get them.

She was wearing a head torch with a red beam as she rummaged in the kiosk.

Nothing behind the broken sliding doors apart from a solitary packet of tobacco. But in the cupboards, underneath was a treasure trove of cigarettes and packets of tobacco. She was stuffing her rucksack when Elijah hissed for attention.

'Not much here, got about 30 beers and two bottles of vodka. John has got some kid's stuff, but that's about it.'

'Okay, round them up and meet me outside in two.'

She gnawed her lip as she stood waiting. They had gotten basically fuck all. As they gathered, she took a beat before explaining her plan.

'John, pick three and go back to the rendezvous. Hold there until then 5:30, and if we're not back by then go back and shove those cigarettes up Greg's arse.

'Don't argue, just go.'

She looked round the rest and with a slight tremor in her voice she issued what she felt was her worst decision in her life.

'Elijah, head into the town along the river path. Look for any bars, off licences, wee shops, anything...' She indicated the five to go with him.

'Rest of us are going up the hill to that smaller store and then see what else we can gather around it. We'll meet here at 4:30. If we don't see you, or vice versa, don't wait, just head straight to the rendezvous and get back safe.'

It was nearly 5:30 when Greg heard the faint signal from the sentry that they were returning. He closed his eyes, wondering if they were all going to be okay. He couldn't contain himself and walked down to the perimeter. As they filed through, he saw the weariness, but also a light in their eyes as they pulled three palettes behind them. He didn't offer any handshakes or back slaps, lest there be casualties. And, he hadn't seen Jenny yet.

But when she did appear, she was holding up an injured man and was dragging two rucksacks behind her.

'I'm glad you're all back,' he said. 'What happened to you?" Pointing to the injured man.'

Before the hobbling Jacob could reply Jenny sighed and said: 'Fell on his arse climbing off the raft - and no, he wasn't at the drink, but he'll need some whiskey to get that bone reset.

While the rest moved up the hill Jenny hung back, bent over, with her hands on her thighs and taking deep breaths. Greg wanted to go over and give her a hug, but he knew that could be misinterpreted, and Sam, Smicker and Seamus were sure to be nearby watching, assessing.

'You okay?' was all he could manage.

'Yeah, wee bit stressed and fucking knackered. But we got plenty of booze, sweets, cheap toys and ciggies, but I saved these for you.'

She took a rucksack from her back and threw it at his feet. He didn't sense any malice in her voice, so he opened it. Inside there were dozens of packets of cigarettes and pouches of tobacco.

'Open the top pocket,' Jenny said as she straightened up. Inside were four packets of cigars.

'Thanks. C'mon' gesturing up the hill.

He sensed that Sam, Smicker and Seamus would be close by.

They sat, looking over where they had first established this camp, smoking cheap cigars, sipping rough brandy. Despite all they might or might not face, for a few precious minutes they were at peace. The dawn's light augured no Ill; the five of them could just be friends enjoying the conclusion of a great night, yet within days they could all be dead, or worse.

It was Seamus who broke the silence first. For once there was no life in his voice. 'We're fucked, aren't we?'

Greg took a deep draw on a cigar, but as he was raising his beer to consider what to say Smicker cut through his contemplation with a harsh tone.

'Why don't you fuck away off! I'll walk you down to the perimeter and watch while you are eaten.'

'Wow, slow down,' said Greg. 'It's been another...well, another one. So long as we can stand together for another hour, another day, and row and fight it means we are the type of people who will not be assimilated or turned…or eaten.'

'You are all deluded cunts. We are fucked, but I'm not going to bend over and wipe my ass and invite them to fuck me up, I'd rather...well, ya know what I mean...'

As Seamus' voice trailed off Greg was thinking about some

considered response, maybe some Churchillian quotation when Jenny and Sam laughed. It was Jenny who spoke first, her face alive with giggles.

'Wud ye all wind yer necks in! We're all just daft cunts trying to stay alive.'

Sam thought how much had changed since she had woken still drunk when the disease hit Northern Ireland hard. She had been so busy studying that she had blanked out the increasingly frantic news reports from Russia, Africa and across Asia. How she had pretty much ignored the advice to wear face masks; how she had accepted the closure of parts of Belfast to stop the spread of the as yet unnamed disease; how she'd been pissed off that some shops had shortages; and how she had had to contact her parents by phone and Facetime only.

Fucking months trying to survive, to just stay alive and not succumb. Now there was hope, albeit slim, that there would be some sort of positive outcome if they all held their nerve.

She, along with six others were on watch, even though they were all still tired from the wait for Jenny's return. And, by her own admission the brandy had gone to her head.

Chapter 6

Four months earlier it had all seemed so easy to just get on with life, reflected Sam.

One mad weekend. Examinations done, hint from two of her tutors that she was a shoe in for a first, and the 'traditional' Northern Ireland attitude of getting fucked up and consuming one's body weight in alcohol in the shortest possible time.

She looked around her and was frightened. Just 22, and being asked to lead, to support, to help and empathise. For fuck sake this North Belfast lass could barely find her way home after nine pints.

But That Morning changed her.

Yep, That Morning was forever capitalised in her mind and would be in any future memories.

A few weeks before she had walked out of the exam hall, picked up the bottle of Buckfast stashed in her gym bag and necked half it. Ohh, fuck, no matter what she got when the scores on the doors were totalled it was over for now with just that interminable time between university and work. Sure, she had worked part time in bars and shops, but a 'proper' job was something she yearned for and terrified her in equal measures.

And then That Morning.

Jesus H. Fucking Christ. It was a cliché, a bitter truth, but that day would be embedded in her mind. Before that, in what seemed a lifetime ago, arrived at the department early, waiting for the Head of Department to pin up the results on the notice board. Her mum had taken the day off, but she'd insisted to her mum not to call until 9:30. If she hadn't got the first everyone expected Sam wanted at least an hour to get completely fucked up.

But as she stood in front of the notice board her name was at the top, not only marked with the rest, awaiting grades noted in alphabetical order but an envelope asking her to attend a departmental meeting in a fortnight's time to 'explore future research paths and publication opportunities' even with the marks yet to be added beside the names. She was anticipating sitting in that room in a few short weeks, the sunshine from the windows catching every dancing mote of dust, the breaths of the three professors, the noise of the traffic on University Street and Botanic. It would be a weird combination of familiarity and trepidation.

Now she was just waiting for her finals result, half nervous, half eager for it. You can be the most confident, talented, polymath but as you stand waiting to find out what you have achieved or not achieved nerves pile up, coursing through every fibre, even with that note hinting at success. It sounded so tried and tested, Sam was self-aware enough to walk away at 10 to nine for a smoke. People around her were gabbling, chittering; some siloed in their own trepidation and some just communicating in monosyllabic responses. She wanted to get back up the stairs to find out what time the interview was set for, even though she had memorised it the first time she read it, and what her actual finals result was, never mind the promised interview. Why they insisted on this archaic system of posting the results on the noticeboard instead of just emailing them mystified her.

So, she had a joint in the early summer morning awaiting what deliberations were to be held in meetings to come but before she got too fucked up perhaps it was time to call her parents.

Her mother was effusive as always, perhaps still holding the pride of her being the first of her side of the family to go to university, and her 'Da'' not being outwardly happy with anything I did as long as I 'pushed myself' to be the best but delighted this time. For once she could detect the pride in his voice. High praise, she thought, for a half-alcoholic author who will probably not be remembered when this planet disappears up its own arse.

CHAPTER 7

'Let's be clear, most of the songs we played during those harrowing days were cathartic, but I don't remember them at all," said Sam, recalling the times when they had songs in their mini convoy. 'When you are scared shitless if you shit it is expected,' she said as she began to explain their journey. Greg had offered an extra double pack of bog roll with a smile rarely seen on his seasoned lips.

As she walked and laughed with 'her' children and those she wanted to care for Sam experienced what was a murderous maternalism and fear.

To become the woman, she was now, was well beyond her comprehension or any rationale...a master's degree, maybe a PhD, maybe even a job; not being one of the leaders of a bunch of survivors who gave the definition of motley crew a run for its money. Her a recently graduated student...fuck she forgot! She had received her result, but she had never actually graduated with all the gown and hat shit, meals with parents and pics in the Belfast Telegraph that each graduate expected.

Could she ever imagined she would be working with an ex-paramilitary, a soldier, a history teacher, a half-psychotic woman, assorted scared survivors and 25 children? PTSD anyone?

She began from her point of view and would let the others fill in their own stories.

That moment when she realised that what had been a distant world crisis came to her door, she was waking up to the worst hangover in what she regarded as the history of the human race.

It has been a three-day bender of epic proportions: pints and shots in the Empire starting the chaos. She would love to be able to recall some of the places they went to, but most of it was a blur; each new day starting with Breakfast Beers, a smattering of food, shared bottles of Buckfast, then on to the serious drinking...

Waking up on That Morning...how the fuck do you face the apocalypse with a hangover? How do you face the fact that your best mate is being eaten by your boyfriend? How do you face having to smack him with a cutting board before stabbing him in the eye? How do you cope with the shock, trauma, horror, grief and pain when you are hungover?

Stumbling out of the flats, throwing up, seeing three 'people' eating a fourth, she stood in an alley, eyes watching the dead-eyed diners tearing at flesh, and shaking. And shaking.

How the fuck did no-one in Northern Ireland not see this coming? What lies were being told by Government here, down south and in London? She remembered the stories of quarantine zones to prevent a pandemic from an unnamed disease, the masks, the police everywhere with the internet equally squealing about zombies on the streets and military rule. Even in the final days between the end of the examinations and her results, she imagined it was somewhere between the two, but the weather was great, there was no sense of panic, army units backing police and not receiving any reaction on the street and some supermarkets without the usual rammed aisles and shelves only slightly sparse. Add in the multitude of conspiracy theories online she just went on with her life.

The supermarkets, however, had not run out of booze.

Piecing it all back together from newspapers collected along the journey it had been inevitable that the zombie plague would come to Britain and then the island of Ireland. The curse of international air travel...

And the curse of those seeing if they can benefit from the end of times. Of course, she didn't piece it all together until they joined with the larger group.

But she still remembered that time, alone and not knowing

what to do, or where to go on That Morning; by then already capitalised it in her mind. Alone, she yearned to be with her mum and dad. She wanted their embrace, their assurance that everything would be okay, she wanted to sit down at the kitchen table with her dad, crack a beer and listen to his warm, if slightly slurred, voice explain all that was going on, how it had come to this, and what was the way out of it, as the smell of her mum's comforting stew slowly coking on the oven surrounded them.

As she emerged from the alley the banquet of the dead was still going on. She turned and walked away as quietly as she could. The long walk-up Station Road had her almost tip toeing, as she looked in every garden, through many windows and down every driveway. Not a living soul, and no body eaters either. Her instincts were that that wouldn't last long. As she neared the end of the road her hangover asserted itself as hunger. Shit, her rumbling stomach might attract the body eaters. No, she knew that wasn't rational, but then again what was?

The shop near the railway station should have some chocolate at least. But it was so dark looking inside she didn't know whether to risk it. Then her stomach grumbled again.

Standing a moment in the doorway her eyes adjusted, and she could see that it was as if it had been ransacked already. But there were still some chocolate bars and bags of crisps, plus packets of headache tablets She began stuffing her pockets until she saw a tiny, child's backpack. Looping it down from a peg she was stuffing as many chocolate bars and packets of crisps it when she heard a low, deep groan from just beyond the doorway. Almost spinning on her heels, she saw what was every cliché from every zombie film and TV show she'd watched with her parents as a young teenager. Slack jawed, grey pallor, tattered clothes and arms outstretched with slack flesh and bony fingertips, and it was stumbling forward towards her. Fuck. Her hand was reaching out around for anything to use, while she kept her gaze on the lumbering form in front of her. A touch, and something metallic: the shop till. With a cry she turned, grabbed it and hurled it to the form that was inches from her. It hit it squarely in the face and it reeled backward, falling. She picked up the old-fashioned cash register and slammed it down on the thing's head. The twitching of the legs stopped.

She sat back, gasping, saw that a grey goo was splattered on her jeans and threw up a little bile. What if she became like the thing she killed? Shaking she grabbed a pile of old newspapers and wiped it off her jeans, jeans she realised she had been wearing for two days and had slept in last night.

She stood trembling, took a breath, and grabbed the tiny, bulging backpack. Could these creatures smell the living, hear noises, or sense the presence of their next still living meal? As she stepped over the body, she realised from the dress it was probably a woman in her late 50s but it could be any age. A brief pang of regret before a ruthless thought that she wouldn't hesitate to do it again. So much for the civilised graduate.

Back in the bright day she began stepping up to the main road when her foot stopped in mid-air. They would be near houses, she was sure. But where wouldn't they be? Like the proverbial lightbulb popping up in comic strips she knew one way, the railway tracks. Quiet, and there looked to be no sign of activity that way. She almost smiled; this was the first time she wouldn't be riding the train on these tracks, gazing at her fellow passengers and looking for any interesting views along a track she travelled almost every day.

It wasn't as easy as it seemed, treading from sleeper to sleeper, or slip sliding along the gravel to the side. She had to stop several times to gobble down chocolate and pain killers to help ease the hangover pain and began wondering when she could get a drink of water. Jesus, the basic essential for life.

What about the infrastructure, the treatment works, pipes...but at least she was dry for now, but it's Northern

Ireland, and would soon enough change, no need to worry about water as it would fall from the sky soon enough…

Smicker picked up the rest of their adventures on the way to Carrickfergus.

As he spoke she ruminated on that part of their journey. Fair play to Smicker, he didn't sugar coat the shit. Especially the time they had both shit themselves. Yeah, Greg's offer of the toilet roll was a worthy nod to that part of the tale he had heard already.

She'd walked as far as the Whiteabbey train station, and it had become too much stumbling along the tracks. No matter the risks she wanted to walk on smooth road for a while. As she finally got up to the road Sam realised that she was walking close to a hospital. Surely it would be a haven for the undead. She was standing, staring, wondering if she should go back to the railway line when she met Smicker. Well, tell the truth and shame the devil, as her da used to say, he scared the shit right out of her. 'It's empty,' he had said pointing at the hospital. She jumped what felt like three feet in the air and tried to get her backpack off her shoulder to throw it at him.

'Woh, woh big girl, don't be attacking this scared wee man,' as a moan echoed in the distance.

That was when both might have touched cloth.

The accent, the half sarcastic tone and the smile in his eyes was enough to bring her heart rate down to pounding as opposed to blast beat intensity.

'Who the fuck are you,' was all she could manage.

CHAPTER 8

Kristin sat in her office wondering why the CIA officers wanted to speak to her so urgently. Secretly the Icelandic government had allowed the Americans to operate a listening post during the Cold War, but it had been scaled back to just two officers, posing as businessmen, as part of the wider CIA network monitoring the chatter that was so beloved of the USA in those years. As a courtesy they visited her once every year and reported nothing. So why now did they want to speak.

Her secretary asked should she show them through, and they walked in looking less self-assured than usual.

'Gentlemen, welcome. Please take a seat.'

They exchanged a glance and sat.

'May I offer you a drink? You look, may I say, nervous.'

'Maybe when you hear what we have to say you'll need a drink too.'

She deliberately took her time, getting three glasses and a bottle Brennivin – the 'native' drink she knew they both had a fondness for - from her desk drawer and poured a generous measure into each glass and said: "Skaal!"

They clinked glasses. As she sat down, she left the drawer open.

She was a small compact woman, with close cropped hair, but she knew that she could pull off the leadership pose and air of assumed authority when needed after three years in post.

'Now, what has you wanting this urgent meeting?'

The older one, Kurt, sat forward, his demeanour still that of the clichéd American middle class. Pressed chinos, white unbuttoned shirt, buzz cut hair and clean shaven.

You've been following the news about the pandemic, I take

it?'

'You know I have,' she replied. 'You listen to everything. You know we have sealed our borders, no flights inbound, anyone arriving on boat is tested, even our fishermen are temperature checked when they return, and we are looking at how we can safely get everyone who is an Icelandic citizen home from abroad. We learned well from Covid.'

'That might not be enough,' said Kurt. 'Not nearly enough.'

His partner, Tim, the younger of the two interjected. 'It's a fucking shit show, and it's getting worse. You need to mobilise whatever military you have.'

'Kurt, Tim, please take it one step at a time if I am to understand what you are saying, and we have no military as such.'

They looked at each other and she realised both were sweating, despite the air conditioning.

'The pandemic,' Kurt said. 'The emmm pandemic isn't emmm, really what it seems. This is going to sound ridiculous, but it is infecting people, killing them and then they come back as zombies.'

She looked at them both, meeting their gazes, sensing that they believed in every word they were saying.

'Well, I've read the ridiculous rumours on the internet, governments' plans to control the population, vaccines, mind control, and even, yes, the undead rising, but surely that is just the conspiracy theorists?'

'I wish,' said Kurt. 'At first Washington thought it might have been a Russian or Chinese biological weapon gone wrong, then we thought it was a virulent coronavirus strain like 2020. Then the reports started coming in across the world. Chatter that was at first dismissed. Until the scientists in the UK, Russia, China and our own all agreed it was really, really fucking bad.

'Then we saw the videos, the pictures and there was no doubt. I've seen two classified videos that show a doctor pronouncing a woman dead. As she was about to be taken to the hospital morgue she literally sat up and bit the neck of a nurse, ripping it open. She went on to kill two others before being smashed in the head by a porter.'

Kristin looked at him.

'I've sent you an email with encrypted videos and files from our labs and some serious shit from the Brits and Russians. I shouldn't have but you have the right to know.'

A question was on her mind, but instead she reached into her drawer and poured three more shots.

'Why did you decide to tell me?'

Tim shuffled a little before downing his drink in one. She poured him another measure and gestured that he should continue.

'What Kurt said is 100% the truth, no bullshit. All the chatter is the same, more and more evidence is coming in about the dead rising whether they have been infected or whatever. It's like a fucking movie but much worse.

'And we think that the spread is getting quicker every day.'

Kurt put his hand on Tim's shaking arm.

'Look, from what we see and the scientists are saying the same thing, there is a neurological infection that literally erases brain function that is associated with what they think is a mutated form of the pervious coronavirus in about 75% of cases but it ignited a hunger that only seems to be sated by human flesh. I would say it was a crock of shit but the evidence is mounting up, and the governments are fucking up.

'Some think they can use it to control their population, some are trying to corral the zombies to use them against opposition groups, some of them are denying it entirely despite the evidence. And, if they had closed all international travel the day they discovered it maybe we could have had a chance.'

Kristin realised for the first time that they were not on some CIA disinformation visit but were being genuine.

'What do you plan,' she said. And, for the first time she

saw a different nervousness in their demeanour.

'Well,' Kurt said. 'We were thinking, well, we are going to arrange a flight back to Washington, and we were sort of thinking, that you here have had a better plan and biosecurity measures than anyone else.'

'Yes,' was all she said, taking another sip of her drink.

Tim spoke up, and she noticed his hand shaking, and more sweat coursing down his face.

'We were sort of hoping we could come back here,' he said. 'Just us, our families and a pilot.'

'Yeah, 20, 25 maximum,' said Kurt.

'Gentlemen, please let me think, it's a lot of information you have just dropped on me here. Who else have you told about your plans?'

'No one, we wanted to get your agreement before we contacted a pilot we trust and get our families organised. We aren't contacting our boss yet, because we see from the chatter that he's started withdrawing staff from offices in Europe and parts of the middle east, probably way too late. We have probably just been an afterthought to date.'

'No one else knows,' Kristin asked again. 'Are you sure?'

They both nodded.

She reached into her drawer. Beside the bottle was a Sig Sauer 9mm pistol that another CIA officer gave her after a brief affair in the late 90s.

Tightening her hand around it, she looked at them both, pulled it from her drawer and shot Tim in the forehead. Kurt simultaneously tried to get out of his chair and reach inside his jacket. The first bullet hit him in the shoulder. He spun, fell and Kirstin walked around the desk to shoot him in the back of the head. She then shot Tim in the head again.

'No one comes here unless we say so,' she said under her breath as her secretary came through the door, taking in the bodies and her blood-spattered prime minister.

'Call the cabinet together now, everyone, no excuses,' she barked. 'When they get here you will join us too.'

Her secretary, shaking with shock, backed away, but Kirstin knew she was going to make the calls.

She wanted to cry, but she couldn't. A trembling hand reached around the desk, and she finished the bottle in two gulps and thought about the blood spattered around her office, on her clothes and on her face.

'It's not like the movies,' she thought to herself and, as she walked to have a shower, sloughed off her clothes and noticed a tear creeping down her cheek.

CHAPTER 9

Three nights before they were set to leave Sam looked round what she'd dubbed the Survivor's Village. When Greg asked her what she meant, she referenced the African proverb 'It takes a village to raise a child'.

'Look around you Greg,' she explained. 'Look at how nearly everyone fusses around the children. Some of the hardest bastards become tender as soon as they go near one of the younger ones. Fuck sake I saw Smicker and Seamus arguing over whose turn it was to change wee Jackie's nappy.

'Tom has been teaching several of them spelling and their times tables. And it worries me.'

Greg looked long and hard at her. 'Why does it worry you?'

'They are attached. All of us are. Having the children around gives us a sense of normality. I'm like the rest of us, really attached to all of them, especially our orphans. But if any of them were to be hurt, or worse, it'll destroy morale at the least or drive the more fragile amongst us over the edge, and then decision-making and discipline will go to hell. You've spent so much time getting us all into shape and preparing us I just…I suppose I'm just getting nervous.'

'That's to be expected,' replied Greg. 'But it's too late now to cancel anything.'

She took a swig from a bottle of bourbon, handed it back and once marvelled at this oddity of a man. He was all skin and bones, and when he was chatting like this, he seemed to be all bundled up in a ball, but when he was addressing any group, or explaining what was being done, and what had to happen he had calm authority that left everyone hanging on what he was saying. Some even took notes. Whether it was true or not he must have been one hell of a teacher.

However, his homely face, could change in an instant, revealing a steely edge, eyes narrowing just slightly, and shoulders pushing back, hands hovering near his waist like some erstwhile western movie sheriff about to draw a six-gun on the bad guy.

'Did I ever tell you about my family, he asked.

'A little.'

'Well, I should tell you a little more then. Anna and I had been married 20 years. Not always smooth, but we always managed a way through without too much trauma.

'When Hal was born we were on the way back to being great, and the unexpected gift of Drew made it a lot better.

'We'd ridden out Covid-19 without any major dramas. When the first of the new lockdowns was announced we agreed that it was best for all if she and the boys stayed with her mother. She had early-stage dementia and had no-one else to care for her, and I needed to finish setting papers for the exam board, and a pile of video calls to pupils.'

He paused, that gesture of pushing his fingers through his hair now so familiar to her, even after such a short time.

'Hal was such a mature young man for a 12-year-old, so studious and interested in finding stuff out. Drew was a more adventurous, mischievous wee rascal. I suppose they both had the best bits of myself and Anna.'

Sam could see the slight wateriness in his eyes and looked away, making a show of lighting a cigarette and reaching for another bottle.

'That's made what I had to do so much harder,' Greg said. "And you need to know what I did. You need to know why being appointed de facto leader is awkward.

'When I saw that shit was getting worse and the lies of government and military were falling apart, I decided to get them out of where they were. It was too close to the exclusion areas, what they called lockdown areas. Not like the 2020 lockdowns, just telling people to stay at home, these were the ones with police patrols and army manning checkpoints.'

'I didn't notice it so much,' said Sam. 'I was too pre-occupied with my degree, results and enjoying the last days of being a student.'

'Oh, they were careful, at first to keep on emphasising the virus but as it all began to unravel the government panicked, closed down or censored news outlets, blocked as many of the stories online as they could, blocked phones and computers from the locked down areas. You would have had to really searched for the truth.

'I was living in a flat of a friend near the city centre, sat one night after a call to Anna and jokes with the boys and decided it was time to get them out, head to our cottage on the north coast, stopping off to pick up my sister and her kids in Ballymena.

'Well, that was the plan. I sat that night drinking; two bottles of wine and fuck knows what else. Made myself some breakfast and rang Anna. She sounded a bit off, as were the boys.

'When I finally got myself together and sat behind the wheel, I thought about the fact that I was unarmed, probably still over the limit to drive and very, very scared.'

'Look if you don't want to tell me, you don't have to,' Sam said, worrying where this story was heading.

'I do, and I'll cut the chase. When I got within half a mile of the house things were in chaos. This must have been just before or just after the bender you spoke about.

'There was an over-turned police Land Rover as I got within a couple of streets from home. As I slowed down to get round it there were the bodies of five cops that looked as if, as the cliché goes, they had been savaged by wild animals. I was shitting myself and thought I needed to get some weapons thinking there would be looters taking advantage, or paramilitaries stepping into the gap.

'Scared as fuck I pulled up close, leant out and grabbed a rifle, a handgun and drove as fast as I could home.

'The door was ajar a window was broken and part of me

just wanted to turn and go. It was more than cowardice. I don't know what it was, but it felt worse than being a chicken.

'Finally, I got out of the car. I looked in the window and I collapsed sobbing. Anna's mother's mauled body was in the corner. Anna and Drew were pulling apart Hal with their hands and teeth. I looked, stared, looked again, stared in what a journalist might say was disbelief, and shot them both.

'Of course, I am not a great shot not having fired a gun in 30 years. They turned and they came at the window. I emptied the handgun and the rifle until they stopped moving. I realised they stopped moving when they were hit in the head.

'It's strange that now I remember the how the guns felt more than my boys' faces. I fired a Glock 17 and then a Heckler and Koch G35. You're the psychologist Sam, walk away or help me understand.'

Instead, she hugged him. She admitted to herself she was confused and worried about her thoughts on Greg – part in love with him, part dismissing it as a crush, part seeing him as a replacement father figure.

'Greg. Greg, listen to me,' she disengaged from the embrace. 'Greg, you've been through more than most here, because it was first-hand. Most of our losses have been remote, even if there is a tiny part of us that hope our families may still be safe.

'You had to confront it. And I'm not really a psychologist yet, just someone who did a degree, but I'm going to tell you what I think. But I'm not going to whisper shit in your ear.

'What you did when you shot Anna and Drew was a mercy killing. They were infected, feral, brain dead and not your family. Consign them to be one of those undead pieces of flesh you freed. You. Did. What. You. Had. To. Do. Remember them as they were, not what they became. Get over it and help us. We're your new family whether you like it or not.'

He stared at her straight in the eye, fixed on what he saw was a young woman who had more leadership qualities and empathy than she could ever realise. He looked at her broad shoulders, narrow waist and long blonde hair - not in any way a sexual way - and considered that all five feet, six inches was packed with potential, if only she would cut down on the booze.

CHAPTER 10

A few days before that she had just finished her rounds with the children, enjoying the lightness and laughter that they had somehow managed, even the ones who had dead eyes a few days before. She claimed she had no favourites but wee Billy, nine years of wired energy. He might have attention deficit disorder, but that energy, inquisitiveness, and downright annoying questioning just made her smile.

She didn't need to walk the boundaries, but she did, to try and ease her questioning mind. Then she smelt what was a familiar scent, grass and not that growing on the fields.

Turning a corner there were Smicker and Seamus sat, each with a massive joint.

'Where the fuck did you get those?'

They turned with the slight, slowness that told her that this wasn't their first spliff of the day.

'C'mon, join us, we've got plenty,' Seamus said. The military precision in his voice gone, his weirdly different coloured eyes watery, and looking more relaxed than she had ever seen.

'Well, when you know a cop it helps,' said Smicker. 'Apparently when Tom hauled his fat ass down to the evidence room, he wasn't just grabbing weapons. He might have grabbed a lot of grass. A fucking shedload, a real shedload.'

He and Seamus giggled. She had never thought they would giggle so openly after all they had been through.

Seamus pulled a lengthy joint from a pocket, lit it and handed it to her. Smicker then reached into a rucksack and handed her one of two bottles of Buckfast.

'We might be fucked, going to die, but we can do it with style,' said Smicker. 'You're turn to order the pizza.'

She sat down between them, comfortable and drew deeply.

'What a time to be alive,' said Seamus. 'What a fucking time.'

'Shut the fuck up you Brit bastard,' Smicker teased again.

'Shut the fuck up you fenian bastard,' Seamus retorted.

They were laughing again at each other.

'Would you two, just for once shut the fuck up,' Sam exclaimed, opening the bottle of Buckfast and drinking deep from it.

They were in the lee of the hill, about 500 yards away from the evening patrols and were in a spot that seemingly had become a blind zone for those wanting a quick sexual encounter in a desperate need to find some intimacy amidst the terror, or those that wanted to get seriously fucked out of their minds.

'I would love to tell you to fuck away off.' said Smicker. 'But you are our leader, I bow to your wisdom, knowledge and baddassery!'

'I'm not your leader,' she said. 'It's just I'm less of a dickhead than you two. And I never break the First Commandment.'

'The First Commandment?' questioned Seamus.

'Yeah, something I read a while back – Don't Be A Dick!'

All three laughed. They needed it right now. The plans for the dash to Ballycastle, then on to Iceland were set, they knew the risks, and they knew of the three of them the odds of coming out alive were slim.

'I'm fucking close to a fucking whitey,' said Smicker. 'But we need to talk.'

Sam looked at him, his shaved head, the squat frame and eyes that were on the verge of tears like so many others in these terrifying times.

'I'm not going,' he said. Seamus and Sam looked to see if he was joking.

'Fuck, I can't forgive myself for what I have done. I can't. You two daft cunts can help, but what I did, I've tried to run away from, I've tried to find God, I've tried to seek help, but I shot a kid in the knees, I've dealt drugs and if I have to die, I'll do it trying to help what little survivors there are. Call it my redemption or whatever, but I'm not changing my mind.'

He sat back, took another drag and swigged from the bottle again.

'I'm not going either,' said Seamus.

'Ahh for fuck sake Seamy,' Smicker laughed. 'I can't do a thing without you copying it.'

"No, I'm serious. You know I was a marine, and what they didn't say in the recruitment ads was that my job was to kill or to be killed. I obeyed orders, that's not an excuse but when they told me I had to, I did.

'Besides I'll help you all get away by blowing shit up.'

It was, Sam thought, the very epitome of an uncomfortable silence. Since she had fled along the railway line Smicker, Seamus, and probably Jenny too had become more than companions amidst the chaos, they had become friends and confidantes.

'I don't know if I can do it without you two eejits.'

Despite being stoned and drunk Smicker turned on her with what was close to anger.

'Yes, you fucking can. No one here can. Greg got this fucked up bunch of wankers this far, but you will… you will take these people to Iceland and whatever the fuck is waiting there, but it will be better than this shit. You don't see it with your hippie long hair, your fucking Slayer t-shirt and, oh so cool combat trousers, but you are the only one.'

It was the only time she had been shocked by Smicker, and she sat back on her hunkers about to swig from the bottle when Seamus simply added: 'What he said.'

CHAPTER 11

When she explained to Greg how they had managed to get to Ballymena she expected disbelief, especially when Jenny, Smicker and Seamus and others withdrew. She was left to outline how they gathered as a small band through wandering.

'It all started when Smicker suggested we try to raid the TA base nearby for guns, she started. 'It was only a10 minute walk away, but when we got there the gates were open but with a makeshift barrier.

'As we approached it, we heard a voice shout 'Halt! Who goes there' like some half-assed line from a war movie.

'Rambo emerged – well he was dressed like some smaller version of Stallone's Rambo. Combat trousers, white vest, red bandana and an ammunition belt slung across his chest.

'Smicker really shouldn't have laughed as Rambo had a pistol pointed at us. But, well you know Smicker, he hides behind his humour.

'When he composed himself, he said 'A wanker and a very angry woman'. As he pointed to me Rambo glanced and Smicker drew a revolver from fuck knows where and pointed it. 'Mexican stand-off mate'.

'I stuttered the daftest phrase. My nerves were still frayed and dried shit on my arse. Why can't we all be friends were the pathetic words, but it worked, and they both dropped their guns to their sides

'Smicker extended his hand and introduced us. Rambo introduced himself as John Jones. He was a squat man, and despite his lean face and muscled arms he had a pronounced beer belly.

'He gestured us in saying 'Fucking hell I'm just glad to see somebody else instead of zombies'.

Greg held up his hand to halt her. She realised she had been telling the story at a mile a minute.

'Slow down Sam," he said. 'I know you want to tell me, but you have got to think as well as explain. It's no use rattling a story off, you have to consider what you want to say.'

'Now I know you were a fucking teacher,' she said, half laughing.

'Yes, but what I wanted as a teacher was to allow my students to explain, not just empty their minds and recite the dates of which king died when.'

'Okay, I suspected something was wrong even before Smicker explained his suspicions.'

Sam went on to explain how Rambo had welcomed them with what seemed like overly effusive gesturing, inviting them into the officers' mess.

'With the major not here, the captain and any others dead here I'm the most senior one left,' Rambo said. 'Lance Corporal Jones, in charge of the entire base, loads of food, loads of booze and scared shitless.' Sam wanted to convey how welcome this seemed at first after her first trek, how the prospect of having people to talk to, sit down in the mess, have a drink that would abate her hangover, but she couldn't quite put it into words.

'I suppose I was still in shock,' she said. 'I had seen what I had seen. That sounds daft, but I was so unaware of what was going on, I was on autopilot even when I was walking along those fucking railway tracks, I couldn't process what was going on.

'Daft wee girl, more concerned with Instragram, drinking and being the dickhead society expected my generation to become."

'Hey, I was young once too,' said Greg. 'We are all dickheads until we die.'

'Yeah, but that was a long time ago in your case.'

She went on to explain how that first night in the TA base they'd ate well – Rambo explaining that he was not a 'real' soldier, just a cook. They'd drank brandy, and he showed them where they could kip. When Rambo was taking a piss it was

Smicker who said 'This place stinks, and in more ways than one'.

The next day, Sam said she awoke from a nightmare, Rambo snoring nearby, but no sign of Smicker. She wandered hoping to find him and see if he had any cigarettes. Every aspect of the base seemed cold; concrete walls and silent, parked vehicles. Eventually she found Smicker throwing up in a corner of a yard.

'You all right?'

'No I'm fucking not – don't look in there if you don't want to barf.'

Even as a young girl if anyone said to her not to look, she would look. She stepped towards where he gestured. She pushed opened the door and felt her bile rising. The room was dark, but the smell of burnt flesh caught her. As her eyes adjusted, she realised that there were at least 10 bodies, all burned, but not so much that it could eradicate all their contorted pain; all the agony they must have endured. The sight drove her back out into the light. Smicker looked grey, she felt she must have looked the same.

'It's a total shitshow, but I need you to go back in before I shoot Rambo in the fucking neck,' he said. 'Look at the two closest to the door. Tell me what you see.'

She'd only known Smicker for less than a day, but she trusted him already, his manner and ease of talking matched with an attitude that suggested more than he wanted to reveal but ask the right question and he would tell.

Taking deep breaths, she steeled herself and walked in again. Breathing through her mouth, she remembered her dad saying, could help stop throwing up, and she did her best, but as she got closer to the bodies the waves of nausea got the better of her. With vomit on her shoes she walked forward and saw what Smicker wanted her to see. The bodies closest to her were face down. They had obviously been shot in the back of the head. She stumbled back from the sight. Almost falling into the daylight he grabbed her and steadied her, and she hugged him, just to know there was still some humanity in the world.

'That wee fuck has some explaining to do.'

She turned to Greg, sighed, and continued.

'Smicker woke Rambo by pushing a gun into his mouth and dragging him upwards with the sight pressing into his upper mouth. He warned him he had exactly one minute to explain why he had executed people.

'Letting the gun slip a couple of inches from his lips Rambo visibly pissed himself. He mumbled and stuttered saying he had to otherwise he would have been dead, and the captain begged him to make sure he wouldn't become one of 'them'.

'He told how all reservists had been recalled, arrested if they didn't, how some English officer arrived to order them to be ready to move and then did what every soldier expected – to wait.'

She looked down at her boots and compressed Rambo's explanation: one of the privates reported being unwell, but before he could be isolated, he bit the lieutenant on the hand before being clubbed unconscious by a sergeant. By then it was too late. Within hours two dozen were showing symptoms and some had begun attacking others. He and the captain had a last stand and finally killed most. A corporal was among the last trying to resist the transformation and the captain shot him in the head, then requested that Lance Corporal Jones show him the same mercy. Rambo admitted he didn't have the guts to do the same to himself.

'Smicker still looked on the verge of emptying every round but was visibly restraining himself. He told Rambo that we were leaving the base in two hours, and he could join us, or not. Rambo begged us to stay, there was plenty of supplies and weapons, but Smicker' expression said enough.

'We loaded up bergens, grabbed as much food and weapons as we could and left.'

Greg looked at his feet as he drew on a cigar.

'Why are you telling me this now, Smicker, Seamus and you have hinted at something about him, but why go into this detail now?'

'Because Rambo is not going to Iceland, he's going to meet with an accident.'

CHAPTER 12

Jenny, Jenny, Jenny, Smicker thought, I could fall in love with you every day. He recalled as Seamus and Sam chattered. He was hoping that she would wander over to where they sat so he could tell her, even though he wouldn't. She was the Amazonian warrior queen and him a wee shit from Belfast would never be worthy of her.

'Shit, this grass is stronger than I thought,' he whispered to himself as the chatter continued.

Tom had joined them and after the cursory slagging of the cop Smicker drifted into his own world, especially remembering how he Sam and Rambo met Jenny.

They had been walking in the middle of the road heading towards Monkstown, Rambo dramatically swinging his SA80 rifle back and forth, after declaring that he would take 'point' and Smicker would have their six. As per our roots, Smicker just declared 'Aye, dead on!' and dandered along regardless.

They heard screaming and a fusillade of swearing. Smicker was the first to react and ran to the source before Sam and Rambo could warn him to stop. At the corner of a street was a lean woman wielding a long stick at two of the undead.

She stabbed one directly in the eye with it and turned to the other one, pulling a large kitchen knife from her waist and stabbing the second one in the mouth. She put her foot straight on the creature's groin and kicked it to the ground, wrestling her knife free.

It was only then she noticed them. Three people that could only be described as having jaws hitting the floor. Even though all carried rifles, she stared before shouting 'don't fucking move'.

Smicker remembering thinking that there was no way they were going to fuck around with this woman. She must have been about five feet four or so, but she looked terrifying.

She marched towards them, and said: 'Right, temperature!', producing a forehead thermometer from a bum bag and systematically taking each of their temperatures in turn declaring them fit 'enough'. Then she broke down in tears. He didn't know what to do, and was about to put his arm around her, before Sam grabbed her in a massive hug.

He looked at Rambo and the man looked as confused as he was.

Her story was so similar to what they would hear over coming weeks, her ex-husband hadn't believed the news about the pandemic and insisted when he had his weekend with their son, and they would go camping up Carnmoney Hill and let the panic blow over.

Smicker thought that must be one brave man, or a completely stupid one.

'Come on over, I'll brew some tea,' she had said leading them to a house just off the main road. In a flash she had transformed from warrior to vulnerable housewife. Which one she really was he didn't know yet.

Over the tea she warned them that she would be taking their temperature every two hours whether they liked it or not. She explained how she had gone to Carnomey Hill to find her son dead, his face half eaten, and her ex-husband nowhere to be found. She buried her only child in a shallow grave and came home to kill anything that she could that was 'less than human and some humans who deserve it'.

Smicker remembered looking at her oval face, framed by dark hair, her body lean and wondering how she had transformed.

It was Rambo who broke the silence: 'How the fuck did you survive with a pointy stick and a knife.'

She half-smiled and went to a cupboard and pulled out an AK47 and a Ruger pistol.

'There's a dead paramilitary who won't miss these.'

'But you were just using…" Sam started.

'Didn't want to waste ammo.'

It broke the tension, and they laughed together, with even Rambo seeming less shifty for once.

She persuaded them to stay that night, after hearing of their plans of where they were headed. He was glad, even after she said that they could only sleep in shifts and take the temperature of the person whose shift came next.

He remembered sitting on a kitchen chair watching the other three sleep on sofas and a camp bed in her living room. Ach, fuck it, tell the truth and shame the devil, he thought Sam and Jenny were two women he wished he had met when he was younger, before darkness took over his life. They were so different, but so alike in their single mindedness. Sam the class swot who would kick your ass, Jenny the yummy mummy who would shoot you in the head if you fucked her off.

Over the coming weeks, when she explained she had been a triathlete, and saw the fury deep inside her, he thought that any army in the world would want her on their side. 'Fucking more terminator than Arnie could ever be.'

Chapter 13

Greg sat two nights before their departure wondering about the people who had assembled here, brought by their messages, and a mix of hope and desperation. Three soldiers, a cop, two computer geeks, a yummy psycho mummy, several mechanical and electrical engineers, and assorted misfits.

He asked Sam what she thought, as ever framing it as if she had more experience in psychology despite having just graduated.

'It's maybe pretty simple,' she said. 'Outside their professions what they did was generally under-appreciated when there were no news stories about them.

'Who notices a cop when there is nothing criminal happening near them, who thinks about soldiers when there is no war, who notices a programmer when they have solved the online problems before they happen, or whatever.

'Those same people are used to living in their bubbles, used to working and coping inside those bubbles and no-one else really understands what they do, many like the geeks, cops and soldiers will have been probably more aware than anyone what was happening thanks to their in-built ability to find stuff out and were, if not prepared, were ready to act in some way.

'As to the others it was luck that kept them alive in the first instance, and then, for whatever reason, they discovered they wanted to survive, or met others that spurred them on.

'See, just a couple of factors.'

Greg's face lightened, a smile halted the glass he was holding inches from his lips.

'I think you know it's a wee bit more complicated than that, but for now that'll do.'

He raised his glass to a toast and once again Sam again

noticed the sadness behind the smile, the way his eyes were downcast when he was planning; when he was thinking; when he didn't want people to see the strain he was under.

'You know they trust you,' he said. "They listen to you, and you have that ability to win consensus.'

'Aye, I just bully them and threaten to take away their booze ration, works every time.'

Greg's sad smile appeared again: 'Yep, that'll work too.'

He looked around where they were sitting. The top of the Norman motte was an impressive height above the surrounding terrain. Much time had been spent cutting down trees to give them a better field of vision. The houses to the south and surrounding streets had been flattened, with a series of controlled explosions that he was shit scared would draw unwelcome attention. Someone said afterwards that it was like a war zone until he reminded them, they were at war. He regretted saying that instantly. Many were still struggling at that point, and they needed to receive the message with care.

He wondered whether Sam's spirit would hold or was her youth going to expire with a sudden breakdown. He doubted it, and that was why he believed having Jenny with her would be a bulwark against any such issue. He thought about the deaths they'd all witnessed, how they had discovered untapped reserves of resilience, but by the same token worried about what would happen when the constant surges of adrenaline faded, when the crash came. Who would be on hand to support the inevitable PTSD that would surge in the group?

'You know what Greg,' Sam said interrupting his train of thought. 'The kids are what will pull a lot of us through. I've heard some of them crying through the night, I've seen others retreat into themselves, but most of what I have seen is the collective group wants to make sure they get a new chance.'

'Aye and get to live off a diet of pickled fish,' replied Greg.

CHAPTER 14

Their destination was Carrickfergus. Sam, Smicker and Rambo had discussed how the old Norman castle, with its walls and sea defence might be the perfect place for other survivors to congregate. Jenny agreed, as she explained the house now had too many memories.

They gathered up their gear, where there was space for extra food in their bergens they packed it in and made sure they had extra ammunition close at hand.

Sam had never been the outdoor type, but the bergen and the webbing felt comfortable despite its weight. All those years at the gym, from she was 16, latterly trying to impress her now dead boyfriend. Thinking back, she was the one making the effort, studying, working out, making the effort that was, only on occasion, reciprocated. Sure, she 'loved him' but she wasn't sure anymore what that meant; was it just a convenient phrase for the first fella she had been serious about?

Too many thoughts crowded in on her, until Smicker shouted: 'Are you away with the fairies?'

Sworn response and they got themselves together to move away from Jenny's house. As they set off Rambo was still acting like he had such deep military experience he would direct the operation. Smicker and Jenny ignored him. She thought that no matter what she would keep a look out on her own terms, as they covered more ground. That was when she spotted Jude standing at the side of the road.

All five feet ten of him, and about 10 stone dripping wet. Lanky with accompanying limp long hair, face so long his chin seemed to be touching the neck of his t-shirt.

'Err,' was all Sam could manage to acknowledge his presence and alert the others.

Of course, Rambo swung his gun round as if confronting an elephant, Smicker kept his pointed at the ground. Jenny, as she expected, marched straight over and took Jude's temperature.

'Bit sweaty but seems okay.'

'Who are you guys,' he managed. Sam thought that he may look shy and a long drink of water, but he was holding a lot within his slender frame."

"We're mad, bad and dangerous to know," said Smicker, immediately setting the young man at ease

Jude's face cracked into a smile so wide it seemed to split his face.

'I'm Jude I just heard voices so presumed you weren't the undead…'

'Well, we're not dead yet, nor undead. I'm Smicker, this is Sam, this is Rambo and this is Jenny. Seriously mate stay on her good side, or you'll get the pointy stick treatment

CHAPTER 15

Tractors. That was Greg's grand plan to get to Ballycastle from Ballymena. 'Fucking tractors,' were Tom's only thoughts. He couldn't believe it, and the man wasn't even a culchie. But as he explained it to what Tom had come to regard as the Inner Circle it sort of made sense.

They were gathered round listening to his plan, some of which he knew, but the others had only pieces like him. He wondered why Greg had been so cautious, but then again Tom recognised that the history man had more than one reason to be cautious.

'Most of you will know that some of the abandoned cars on the dual carriageway are fit for use, but even the 4x4s can't be relied on across rough terrain. We have just enough vehicles, but we don't have the means to make sure they can manage the journey, especially the mini-buses and school buses for the children," he said.

'We need to get at least four tractors. We have two nearby to date, so I need some of you to go out on a recon to see if there are others, close, or else we may be in trouble in meeting the deadline.

'The idea is that if any of the vehicles gets stuck the tractor can pull them out, or even just tow them. Also, the two have space in their cabin to mount guns…carve a path if needed.'

He paused and Tom looked round. Smicker had the look of a man who didn't want to be within miles of an agricultural vehicle, Sam, as always deep in thought, Seamus seemed to be considering how to mount the guns, and Jude spoke up.

'I think I know where we can find some tractors.'

Everyone looked at him.

'Err, what I mean is my cousin worked at a place that sells them. It's about a 15-minute drive from here.'

'Well, if we can get them there that would be a weight off my mind,' said Greg. 'As you know there's a lot more to the plan than that, but it would be massive if we can get them, but let's not count our chickens.'

Tom looked closely at Greg and pondered again at how he had become the de facto leader, his immense knowledge of military strategy and tactics and his ability to take on and accept or adapt what ideas others might have. Even the former soldiers deferred to him. There was a calm authority to the man that he probably didn't even realise he had.

After all it had been Greg's idea to establish their mini refuge on this ancient motte and bailey, something Tom had only ever seen driving by it, but never taking any real notice of.

When the first merry band had been persuaded to encamp there, it was plain from the off that it was as ideal in the 21st Century as it was in the 12th Century. Apart from being on the high ground, clearing the trees and demolishing most of the houses nearby had given an almost perfect field of vision. That with the scavenging of anything useful from the houses had been done with care and thought. Tom, even as a cop, had been amazed at how many weapons they had found hidden in cupboards and under beds before he remembered this was Northern Ireland, after all.

Their resident geek, Mark, was the one who had come up with the idea of scavenging solar lights' rechargeable batteries to power radios, walkie talkies and then the night vision glasses that Simon had brought. As well as Mark's own device that could take down drones.

He remembered the first time Simon had come into the camp, sneaking past all the traps, apparently crawling along until he had a gun in Greg's face whispering that he had been watching them for days and wanted to know whether they were working with anyone. Greg had simply told him no and stood up. That was enough for Simon and he holstered his weapon.

Chapter 16

Simon was a strange one, a fact he readily admitted, but he also recognised that Greg had a strange authority around the camp and deferred to him.

He told them that he was sort of military and Greg quietly said 'I'm guessing that reconnaissance was something you specialised in.'

'Pretty close.'

Simon was a squat-looking man despite his height, looked rugged, but was also lithe in his movements and had a jawline any A-lister star would envy. Greg's assessment was that behind the slow, low sentences the man would also kill without hesitation even as he weighed up what he was saying.

His tale had been much like the others, even if it first seemed strange to hear such a clear English accent.

Simon's 'unit' as he described it had been designated to Northern Ireland as he was familiar with it, while others had been deployed across the British Isles.

They had been tasked with supporting other military units and would be briefed when they arrived. That was when his world fell apart.

'We were called into a briefing at a police base near Carrick,' he explained. 'When we arrived my gut was churning. Way too many soldiers, but not that many belonging to a single unit, more a rag tag mixture of regiments and a hardman general in charge.

'After settling in I asked why the car park had a steel fence and screens around when some wee jumped-up captain told me he would issue orders and explain then momentarily. I outranked him – yes, I am a major, albeit young for the rank – but didn't need the hassle of calling him out.

'And don't worry I'm not going to try and lead or issue

orders, you seem well organised here. Suffice to say the orders were not ones I was inclined to follow.

'I'm sure you can guess, control the civilian population, use the zombies if needed in small groups to instil terror and compliance. That's when one of the pricks in charge showed us the CCTV view of the car park with 20 or so undead wandering around, trying to clamber out.

'I couldn't do it. Look, I have been in the army long enough to recognise shit orders, but this was too much, too uncontrolled and too many risks. So, I simply slipped away with my, err colleague.'

Tom couldn't help himself: 'Aye, and I bet it wasn't too difficult for a man like you, sneaky and all that.'

Greg shushed him, and again tried to assess what this Major's real skillset, and it was when for the first time he noticed the deep, dark shadows around his eyes, the worry lines around his mouth. Everyone around the motte had dark shadows but for some reason this man's features seemed hollowed out.

'I'm guessing you had a rough ride getting here,' he said. Simon just nodded.

What was clear, soon after that he arrived Major Simon became, almost an aide de camp for Greg, listening to what he wanted, suggesting minor improvements, implementing them and never demeaning anyone that didn't understand.

That was until the night he disappeared, and Greg couldn't explain that disappearance, nor the nagging fear that he would be reporting to some higher authority. From all the messages they had heard, all the tales of survivors, and the evidence to hand it was clear that some in the military, or whoever was issuing orders, that they still wanted to use the zombies to instil fear, gain control, without noticing that the situation had already gone beyond anyone's ability to control. And, he suspected the major was telling half-truths about the situation in Carrick.

He couldn't worry too much about the disappearance of

Simon right now – after all he had left most of his equipment - but it still played on his thinking, and final refinements to the plan may be needed. Plus, he wasn't sure Simon had been telling everything about his journey.

Chapter 17

By the time they reached the outskirts of Carrick Sam and her merry band of survivors numbered 11. After they bumped into Jude it seemed that every mile or so some bedraggled person, looking at them with a mixture of hope, fear and desperation. And, in each case Jenny took their temperature and asked did they have any spare batteries.

Smicker, as always with a lack of tact that bordered on the ridiculous, but his charm helped him get away with crudity, said: 'Aye, we need some for the torches but you must have a fucking vibrator running on maximum every night'.

Jenny somehow managed to laugh and scowl at the same time. A tall, black man with lengthy dreadlocks, just looked on with bemusement, and spoke with one of the broadest Belfast accents ever heard.

'Errmm, I'm Elijah, and while I'm glad to see you, what the fuck are ye lot talking about.'

'Don't worry about it mate, just glad to add to our merry bunch of wanderers.

Elijah's tale was like most of what they had heard, surprised by the speed of the whole thing, one minute worried about the pandemic next the fucking army and the undead seeming to be competing in spreading fear, just the army was pretending to know what it was doing.

The round of introductions, sharing out weapons, ammunition, food and water. Somehow Jacob had managed along the way to scavenge beer, and despite a semi-futile argument that they were already carrying too much, they all had relented and added them to their bergens.

'Here big lad, here's a can of lukewarm beer,' he said, handing one to Elijah. In just about two swallows he downed the entire can. 'Fuck I needed that," he said, wiping his mouth.

'Don't suppose any of you fancy some Buckfast?'

The entire party drooled at once, before Sam spoke up: 'Yes, but you lot take it easy on it, no jungle juice sessions.'

They were on the outskirts of Carrick by that stage and had sat up their evening camp, as always in the fields at the edge of the road, with dedicated watches throughout the hours of darkness. Smicker and Sam had taken on the roles of allocating these and despite the occasional grumbles from Rambo they were mostly stuck to.

It was that night that Sam woke to Andy gently tapping on her shoulder.

'We're being watched,' he whispered. Sam shook Smicker, holding a finger over her lips. He nodded and drew his gun.

'Over my shoulder, about 30 yards or so,' Andy explained. Rising with care, Sam and Smicker began a spurious conversation about changing rotas and walked to where Andy had pointed as Andy circulated the tents waking everybody.

Sam caught movement to her left, indicated to Smicker and walked with purpose to the spot.

'Can we help you?' sounded stupid as soon as it left her lips, a throwback to when manners and civil discourse seemed important.

A tall, hefty woman stood up, and behind her a slender, sickly-looking girl barely in her teens.

'If you have some food, we'd be very grateful,' the stout woman said. 'I'm Julie, this is Ruth.'

'C'mon, you're more than welcome.'

Their tale was a little different from the rest of their party but still had haunting reminders for all of them. Julie had been scouring social media for weeks before society went tits up. By her own admission she had believed every conspiracy theory, posted on anti-mask sites, and had been firmly anti-vaccinations of any kind during the 2020 pandemic. She had barely left the house for a couple of months, surviving, in her own words on "takeaways and paranoia". When her mother fell ill, they had tried to call the doctor, but as in so many cases the doctors were either overloaded, or ill themselves. She tried calling helplines, to no avail.

'By the time I tried calling the hospitals I saw mum getting close to, you know, dying,' Julie explained. 'I was just trying to get her settled one night and trying to drink something when she died, that, you know, final breath. I couldn't find a pulse and I just sat on the side of the bed. There were no tears then. I don't know why.

'I don't know how long, but as I was about to stand up, she grabbed me…'

Ruth hugged in tight to her and Julie just stood trembling.

'She tried to bite me, and I just got free and ran. I would have ran until I collapsed if I hadn't met this wee girl.'

They had been wandering for a week, surviving off scraps from kitchens but feeling as if they were near starved. Sam sensed that had Julie not bumped into Ruth she never would have made it. It was as if they were sisters, but the teenager was the eldest.

She refused to explain how she had survived the initial waves, just saying 'I'm here, that's enough'.

Sam wondered what was behind this lean teen's dark eyes, and why she felt wary of Julie

Chapter 18

Greg was sitting on his own, at peace for once. They were on the verge of departure, and he knew he had to put aside his anxiety. More worry would not help.

The darkest hour comes before dawn was the perfect description as to where they were at, and what was in the immediate future. The variables were immense, but they could only control so much. He, for a change, wasn't going to numb himself with whiskey, content to have a couple of warm beers, knowing he needed a clear head in coming days.

Somehow, he had managed a few hours' sleep, perhaps comforted by the discovery of Simon's supplies. Handguns, ammunition, field rations and one of the two sniper rifles he had. That, and the enigmatic note: 'Don't trust me, but I have your backs'.

You could imply much, but Greg believed it meant, in the best possible light, that Simon was working with some branch of the army still but wasn't about to betray their plans. Hopeful thinking, but hope was where you chose to find it.

He had given his final speech – fuck he hated that he had to, but they expected something from him and he was yet to figure out why. He had wanted them all to feel that same hope, wanted the inner circle to feel that they should pass on that same hope to everyone, wanted them to believe it was more than a 50 50 chance, and maybe then they would fight harder to survive.

That inner circle had become more important to him than any had been in his professional career. In different circumstances he would have been proud to have them call him a friend. Their flaws were out on display, and in their own ways had tried, over the previous weeks, to do their best to address them.

Samantha – she hated when he used her full name – had become mature beyond her years. Maybe it was her psychology degree lessons steeped deep inside, or maybe it was just her character. She had tried over the previous days to keep off the drink, but he suspected what was before just a student habit had become a serious and dangerous coping mechanism.

As to Smicker and Seamus. The odd couple. A Royal Marine commando and an ex-paramilitary who had become close friends; both damaged by their past, both willing to do what they could to redeem themselves. And, Jenny, programmed somewhere deep in her DNA to be a warrior. Then big Tom, wry humour aside he had, for some reason become the de facto leader for the children and teens, who followed him, and he never lost patience with a single one of them.

He ran through them all, all he had come to know, and all those who had came to this site.

And all he could manage in his final speech to them was: 'Imagine the worst that can happen. Imagine the best that can happen. Prepare for both and somewhere in the middle will be the reality we have to face.'

Fucking pathetic, but it would have to do – he was out of Churchillian quotations, and he doubted that Ancient Greek tales about Sparta would help – after all the 300 were all killed at Thermopalyae.

The hope that they had in Iceland and the only lie that Kirstin had told them, that there were no conditions. Then the calm announcement that anyone over 50, and anyone with a chronic medical condition were not welcome. He could understand it. He was over 50, and had mild arrythmia, not to mention pre-diabetes and a serious addiction to smoking. Yes, he would be a liability to any health service even in the best of times.

He knew that he had to get them just to Ballycastle then he would decide his own path along with Smicker and Seamus and those nine others who had been deemed not healthy or young enough to be welcomed.

CHAPTER 19

They were within a mile of Carrick Castle when everyone in their party started to get nervous. There were no visible signs, but there were noises in the distance that sounded like an entire football stadium was muttering. They had slowed to a crawl, when Smicker motioned to Sam.

He said: 'There is something here I don't fucking like. I'm thinking this wasn't such a good idea. If we thought about the castle, a lot were maybe thinking the same – a fucking load more than we expected.'

Sam looked down the road they were on. The houses looked to have been abandoned for years, and the cars seemed about to sink on their axles, even though it had just been such a short time since the world went to shit.

She was about to tell Smicker that they should at least go a little further when a man in full military fatigues stepped from behind a tree. He had his arms aloft and walked slowly towards them. Rambo as usual took it as a threat until Smicker gently pushed the barrel of the rifle down, whispering 'Let's just see what he has to say'.

What he said crushed their hopes of safety in the Norman castle, but at the same time offered options.

'Let me just say that I barely got out of there,' he began. 'The plan was to secure the castle, establish a perimeter around the police base at Sea Park and control the influx of civilians to the town. That did not work.'

Sam noticed the precise sentences, measured tones, and, beneath the baggy fatigues, a body fine-tuned for combat. His stubbly beard the only thing not screaming of army demeanour.

'I do not need or want to be near any of those pretending to be in charge,' he said. 'By the way my name is Seamus, and the part of the regiment I came from does not use surnames.'

Smicker interrupted with his usual decorum: 'Got any cigarettes?'

'Aye, I do indeed. You got any beer?'

He accepted a can and explained that he had somewhere to go and explained how and why.

'I'm going to get hold of a radio, maybe the people with the radio won't want me to have it, and then I have somewhere else to go. You may not want to join me when you hear where it is.'

Jenny volunteered to go help, as did Smicker. Seamus eyed them. Smicker just said: 'Tell you what mate, this wee woman Jenny would kick your arse into tha marra, then Sam here would kick it back into today, soldier or not, so we comin' on then.'

Smicker had been reluctant to talk about what the trio had done to get hold of three radios and other kit, as was Jenny. Seamus only offered a short 'we did some stuff to get them'.

A beer and cigarette later he explained the plan he had.

'Some of the higher ups have been monitoring civilian refugee's transmissions. One of them appears better organised than others, with structures and defences. They were on the verge of sending a squad, with caged zombies and all, up to it to round up the group to see who was in charge and what they planned. I read that as to eliminate any threat to martial law but before they could issue orders things went to shit. What was it they said about 2020? A total shit show. Well, that is what it is like down there only worse. Civilians breached the barricades, confused soldiers didn't know whether to shoot or not and zombies were in the midst of it all. Some people got away on boats, some didn't."

'Aye, it looks a right shambles and we weren't any way close,' said Smicker. Jenny nodded and took a swallow from her beer.

Sam looked at them, her motley crew. 'First order of the day is to find somewhere to rest up, get some food and maybe have a chinwag then.'

'Who died and made you Elvis,' Smicker said.

CHAPTER 20

The plan was simple, at least it sounded simple. Greg appreciated that there were many pitfalls. Many a slip between spoon and lip, his mother would have said.

Take two school buses, for minibuses, six four by fours as far along the motorway and dual carriageways as possible. If they needed to go off road the tractors could tow them, as well as clearing any obstacles. He still didn't quite know how Jude came up with the idea of borrowing a snow plough blade from the Road Service depot, but it had solved one part of the journey's puzzle, getting through motorway barriers, dense hedges and any obstacles in fields, a little like how the Allies had used bulldozer blades on Shermn tanka in the Bocage of Normandy in 1944.

There were other puzzles that would need solved as they went, too many to worry about right now.

What would normally be just over half an hour's journey needed to be planned as a full day plus an extra two hours for any changes or obstacles. Add into that the unpredictability of travelling with children. Tom forecasted at least one hundred cries of 'Are we there yet' and two dozen calls about needing to go to the toilet. Greg thought he was erring on the low side, but then again, the children trusted Tom so much he reckoned they might listen to him when he asked them to shush. Food stops, detours, using costal roads and being aware of potential ambushes all had to be factored in.

He had to be reminded by Seamus not to use jargon when he said that we needed to add more ammunition at the L&D.

'For fuck sake, they don't know what that means, and I'm surprised anyone outside the army knows what that means,' he had said. 'For those that need an interpreter yer man means Logistics and Distribution, or what you lot call 'all them the cars over there'.

It broke any tensions that lingered.

He was going to go over the routes again and again with them to make sure there were no doubts. Two different convoys, one on the motorway and then dual carriageways, one on the coastal road. Greg's 'teams' would drive a little along the motorway and a little along the coastal route to provide support, and if necessary, lend firepower.

This was the part of the plan had the most worries for him. The two Land Rovers they had would be at least 20 minutes away from the other column should they need assistance, and that was presuming they could get a radio message through, given the hilly nature of the terrain at any one time. He had to be brutal with them in his assessment.

'Look, there is a high probability that one of our columns won't make it. We can cause as much a distraction as possible and fight to let any one group reach Ballycastle, but I can't say for sure there won't be a period when you will have to stand on your own. If it's military, we won't be much use in a straight up firefight. If it's a swarm of zombies, we may not be able to help either. All we may be able to do is save some....'

Sam wandered off from the briefing, she knew all the plans and risks. She was taking the column along the coastal roads, while Jenny would lead the column that had a few miles of motorway before she would be on dual carriageways then country roads too.

Sam's was possibly the more difficult part of the journey. Heading down treacherous roads at the best of times to Glenarm, down the glen then the winding coast, with roads that wouldn't be wide enough to skirt past - hills on one side, sea on the other. Sure, there were alternative roads up the glens, but many would involve doubling back, costing time and increasing risks. Jenny would have a hairy time going through Ballymoney, but if she got through there she should be in the clear.

She was mulling this over when Seamus gently tapped her

shoulder.

'I'd tell you to stop worrying but there's no point, we're all worrying,' he said. 'You can run this over in your mind as much as you want, but we are as set as we will ever be. An old Prussian general, Von Moltke I think, said plans disappear with the first contact with the enemy. In other words, it will all go to fucking pieces any way once it starts but you can adapt, change plans when you need to, but you can't run through every possibility.

'You will find a way. If you have to lead the children up a mountain or through a river on foot you will have to do that, even if you have to pull them through using a wire cutter and a piece of string…'

'Fuck up Seamus," she interrupted him 'I know that is the way you marines were taught, but I haven't had years of experience and training, I was just a daft wee student until a few weeks ago.'

'You are anything but daft, and you can do more than you expect. This isn't a pep talk; this is an honest assessment. You lead well, you are fitter probably than you have ever been in your life, you're not the greatest shot, but you understand that if you lay down enough fire it allows others to escape, or to get a better shot.'

'Oh fuck," Sam replied. 'Has a Royal Marine Commando just given me some half-assed sandwich feedback? Some strengths, some weaknesses, and finish with a strength to make me feel better? Well, I never, oh deary old me, there's a first time for everything.'

'Shut up, will you please. That wasn't what I meant, and if it came across as patronising, I'm sorry. Do you remember when we had our first proper chinwag outside Carrick?"

CHAPTER 21

They had found an abandoned filling station with attached shop at the top road on the outskirts of Carrick, and after scouting out the surroundings, settled in to eat. Of course, before that Elijah and Smicker had checked out the neighbouring cricket club and returned with dozens of bottles of beer, Smicker loudly declaring that as bottles were too heavy to carry, they would have to drink most of them tonight.

Despite most wanting to hear what Seamus had to say they were right now too hungry. Buttered bread, tins of tuna, sausages cooked on an open fire, potatoes wrapped in foil on the same fire roasting, and as much chocolate being eaten that would be consumed by a small town at Christmas.

Smicker burped loudly, very loudly. Rambo even went to reach for his weapon.

'I guess that's my cue to explain,' Seamus said. Almost at the same time Sam, Smicker, Jenny and a few others lit up cigarettes. Ready, yet nervous, for what this soldier would explain about their future plans.

'The area I was tasked to 'assess' before I all went tits up at the castle was in Ballymena, specifically an ancient motte and bailey. Drone footage showed that there were well established defences, camouflage and what appeared to be clearing of adjoining houses,' Seamus went on. 'I suspect I wasn't the only one sent.

'Yet every time an image was being downloaded the drones would fail, signal lost, no further downloads. Also there appeared to be coded radio signals coming from the same location.'

'Has anyone here heard of Stiff Little Fingers, Pink Floyd or The Clash?'

A few nodded, some of the younger ones looked blank.

'The signals played, in order, SLF's Alternative Ulster, The Clash's London Calling and Pink Floyd's Is There Anybody Out There, followed by a simple 'Bout Ye, gizza bell!'

'A few local soldiers got the SLF reference, but not all did get The Clash or Floyd songs. Thankfully my family were all rockers or punks, so it was easy to work out, even if the senior officers were baffled.'

Sam said: 'It's so fucking simple, are they that daft.'

'Woah there, missus brainy pants, as a long-standing resident of north Belfast I get SLF's Alternative Ulster, but how does it all link,' said Smicker.

'Ach for fuck sake man, it's easy,' Sam replied. 'This is where they have an alternative Ulster, there's a line in London Calling, oh never mind about that, it's just calling out, and the Pink Floyd song it has Is There Anybody Out There repeated, you said four times Seamus, and then a simple call us message.'

'Fucking hippy,' Smicker replied.

'The point is that whether they are setting up some sort of alternative government, desperate for supplies, or just want company they seem better organised than the fuckers down there, or in any part of Ireland or Britain, believe me I've heard and seen the reports, the video and heard many messages – none of which seems as planned as this.

'So, what do we do, catch a helicopter and bop up there,' said Smicker and was about to go on, until a well-aimed sausage from Jenny landed in his lap.

'Ahh, fer fuck sake woman!'

'Smicker, fuck up. Elijah if he opens his mouth again feel free to shove a hot sausage up his arse sideways, no lube. Now, please continue Seamus…'

Even the hard face of the marine couldn't resist a smile, which became a grin and soon everyone was either giggling or laughing. It was what they needed, and part of Sam wondered if Smicker was setting up the put downs, making the deliberately daft comments or was just that type of person who instinctively had to have something to say. Fuck, she would have to stop trying to analyse people.

The laughter died down and Seamus composed himself.

'We could be in Ballymena in much less than a day or so by road,' he said. 'As you know we went out and got radios. If we were to contact this group and see if they will accept us, we can try and jump start at least three cars and take the back roads there.

'That might not be possible, but the back roads have less populated areas, and less potential outbreaks, military checkpoints or worse. And, if we are forced to go by foot these wee babies will help.'

He presented them with three squat devices, just a bit larger than a mobile phone, but looking much more rugged.

'I give to you the latest army issue GPS devices," he said. 'I may have liberated these from some people who will have no use for them any further.'

'How can they work when our mobiles don't,' asked Ruth.

'Your mobile relies on cell towers, and a whole lot more including electricity, but the satellites are still up there, and these things have that sole purpose of telling you, with the help of those same satellites, where you are and a scrolling map to point to where you want to go. Not easy to use at first but believe me they are very accurate and useful.'

'Well, I guess you need someone to hotwire some cars then,' said Smicker. 'As long as it can wait til the morning, as I think I may be over the limit, and I don't want to lose my licence if the cops come back.

Chapter 22

The evening before the rush to Ballycastle seemed to last forever for everyone, including the increasingly restless children and young people. One concerned Greg and Sam more than anyone else. JoJo.

The 15-year-old was obviously intelligent and able, not least how he made his way from Bellaghy to Ballymena without a single wound or any obvious mental scars, but plenty of tales that in other circumstances would have been remarkable but were probably true.

He had confided to Greg and Sam separately that he felt useless just tagging along with the children to 'keep an eye on them' and wanted to fight if it was needed.

Greg had been thinking of some limited role, but Sam was implacable, a new society should not have child soldiers.

'Yes, he's big for his age, yes he has been shown how to handle a weapon by Seamus and Tom, yes he's smart and yes, he probably could defend himself and others, but if this is to be a new society we shouldn't start with compromises,' she argued.

'Not too long ago people JoJo's age would have been fighting with regular armies across the world,' Greg said. 'It was only late in the 19th Century that there were age limits set in most countries. Before that, if you could lift a rifle, or load a canon you were enlisted, or press-ganged into the navy.'

'That's why we changed things,' Sam said, raising her voice. 'We don't want children becoming used to wielding a gun, we don't want them to have to deal with killing someone. There was too much of that in shitholes across the world we should be setting a better example for the future.'

They sat in silence. They both knew they were right and wrong at the same time given the circumstances they were facing, a world that was gone to hell in a handbasket.

Eyes downcast, neither wanting to look at the other. At the same time, they lit a cigarette and momentarily glanced at each other. The confused feelings Sam had for Greg came to the fore. He was someone she had grown to respect, a father figure that in different circumstances she would have willingly had as a lover, despite the age difference, and his otherworldly knowledge of military history. She decided to change tack.

'You know so much about fighting, why did you never join up?'

'They would have made me cut my hair,' he said. 'I was quite the wee rocker and metalhead in the 80s. And I was never good at taking orders from people who knew less than me. Yeah, I was an arrogant wee prick. Took me until I was 25, flitting from job to job that I realised that I could do something useful.

'That was when I became obsessed with wars. Teachers, off over the summer, and daytime documentaries dripping with the tales of World War Two, how Hitler rose to power, how the war was fought, and I slowly realised that I knew more than the so-called historians and producers of those shows, and I read more and sought out the primary sources. Traced my own family's service records back to the Great War and even the Boer Wars. I even thought about writing my own historical tome, but…well family, job, laziness took over.

'But you make a good point. That's the shrink in you, I learned and learned never knowing that it would be useful. And you steered the conversation away from JoJo.'

'Yeah, I was giving myself sometime to think. There may be a compromise.'

'I'm all ears.'

'I don't like it, but if it solves anything we can give him a rifle with one round loaded and a full clip at hand, but it is the understanding that his role is to assist Tom in protecting the children in his column, and not to engage anything or anyone without Tom giving orders.'

'And I suppose you want me to explain that to them both?'

'Yes, oh mighty leader.'

'But what about the pointy sticks?' he said.

A week ago, Smicker had asked for a couple to search for brush shafts, and when he had collected a dozen he cut them in half and sharpened one end.

'Oh, fuck I nearly forgot about that,' Sam laughed. 'I'm still not sure.'

Smicker planned to give any of the older children and younger teens a pointy stick to use if their vehicle was surrounded.

'It's a good idea to give them a sort of weaponised comfort blanket, but as they say it's all fun and games until somebody loses an eye.'

Chapter 23

The initial stage of the journey to Ballymena was a lot more straightforward than any of their party had anticipated. And surprisingly the marine and the former paramilitary became more than just acquaintances thrown together through circumstance. They became close, more than friendship and banter, but it was something Sam saw was a bond. Brothers in arms it may have been, but they relied on the slagging and banter to keep themselves level amidst the chaos.

She was sitting at the edge of the road, half into the woods, half out, watching the people she was with. They had taken a break from the drive to allow everyone, especially those who had been driving, some time to rest, eat and, for her to think.

Like a vision from some romantic 19th Century poet the sunlight was dappled through the trees. The ground was soft with pine needles, the temperature moderate, yet just warm enough not to feel uncomfortable for the time of year. She was beginning to doze, what sleep she had caught was not enough, when she caught movement. At the edge of the road, she saw Julie and Ruth walking towards Rambo. He turned and was more effusive in his conversation than he ever would have been with anyone else. There was gesticulation, smiles and even laughter, until Mervyn walked by. Then it was silence.

Fuck I am becoming even more paranoid, she thought. Given any other circumstances such suspicions would not have bothered her, but under this benighted summer day all her senses were more alive than ever. The light through the trees, the sound of a nearby stream, the soft clicking of a cooling engine, the light chatter of those in the group, the sound of footsteps around her. And a weird thought cascading into her mind: where does anyone take a shit in a pandemic?

She stood, and dandered across to Smicker and Seamus.

‘‘Wee quest'on for you two,’ she said. ‘Did any of you think to grab bog roll when we were at the garage?’

‘Wipe yer wee sweet arse on leaves,’ Smicker said with his usual diplomacy.

‘Fuck up you daft cunt. We are all a little ripe. I could smell the two of you a mile off, and if I can smell your pits and ball sacks, then sure as shit the fucking zombies will smell you too. We need to think about some way to get everyone cleaned up, and maybe even a change of clothes.’

‘Fuck! I never thought about that. There is a village about four miles ahead,’ said Seamus. ‘We can try there for some essentials, even if it's only some body spray for Smicker.’

Chapter 24

Rambo, or as Greg increasingly thought of him as Corporal Jones, from the ancient Dad's Army TV show, had become increasingly irritating, as the days counted down to the departure. Sam's assertion that he would have an 'accident' before they departed still lingered in his mind. Yes, he didn't doubt she could kill him, but was that something she could live with? She was a leader, yes, but could she, would she, want that burden? And how would she deal with Julie? At every step Julie had begun to question every decision he had taken and everything that the lead group had decided. As he sucked deeply on a cigar, he thought he should set Jenny on her, but that came under the category of cruel and unusual punishments.

They, to his mind, were the wildcards in the planning, not to mention the awkward teenager, Ruth. Their concerns might, or might not be, legitimate but everything he had thought about since that first call from Iceland had been to get as many safely away as possible.

He pulled the old combat jacket close around him, remembering when he had bought it from a second-hand store in Belfast more than three decades ago, knowing that he still fitted into it because of his illnesses, and knowing that in all probability he would die in it. All, while wondering why he had thrown it into the boot of the car before leaving his house to live in a flat when the new pandemic descended.

There was comfort in the old coat, memories of being socially awkward, overcompensating, going to gigs, stashing beers in its inner confines and feeling, if not cool, at least fitting in. At that time in the latter years of his teens he had behaved in a more outlandish manner than a younger him may have ever contemplated, yet he knew it was because he, like most other children and teens, wanted to just fit in, never mind that he chose to fit in with punks and metalheads – they didn't seem to judge as long as you knew the words to the songs.

He realised he was prevaricating using a long-held suspicion that he was some sort of outsider, and since people had gathered here, he had at times been overwhelmed by feelings of imposter syndrome. He was just coping with the situation and hunkering down when people started asking him 'what to do'.

Driving out of Belfast he had soon had to leave the motorway, because of crashed and abandoned cars, and while on the Antrim Road he had spotted a woman and child crouched in a garden. He stopped and walked slowly over, assuring them he was not a threat. After a few minutes coaxing they agreed to going with him.

By the time they had neared Ballymena the car had six passengers packed in. At least the police wouldn't be pulling him over for being over-loaded.

When they got to his sister's house it was burned out, along with several others in the terrace. Exhausted, physically and emotionally, he needed to stop. They were near the Norman motte and bailey, and all he could think of was to stop somewhere to rest that they would be on high ground to see anything that may approach.

Was it just because he had been the driver that he became de facto leader? Or was it just him slipping into teacher mode, asking leading questions to learn about their abilities and how they are feeling?

Sitting at the base of the mound he wanted to just sleep, his actions when faced with his family re-surfaced, now he was not concentrating on driving. Fuck he was tired, but for the first time the tears welled up. He sobbed, and his nostrils filled up – that awful feeling that he was about to become out of control.

'Errr, Greg, you okay?' said Jeanette, the woman he had

first picked up with her young daughter.

'Aye, just a lot going on.'

'Yeah, a lot…are you hungry, because I don't think anyone has eaten much.'

They were looking to him to think of something and an anger rose, as if he had all the answers, but like when a pupil wound him up, he swallowed his irritation. He was hungry too, and tried to remember nearby shops, but he was wary of the supermarkets he could see on either side of the motte and its surrounding grass slopes.

'Tell you what, if you can organise a few people to watch I can drive to a shop and see what I can get,' he said. "Anything you see that's not quite human, go through that gap behind me, the one with the children's swings, and I'll look for you heading along the road when I get back.'

The filling station and its shop were deserted, apart from a severed arm near the diary cabinet, and he filled two shopping trolleys with as much as he could think could be easily consumed. After he packed them into the car, he returned to grab what cigarettes there were. He had stopped years ago, but he didn't think any of their long-term health would be measured in decades.

Later that day, when Tom casually dandered up the hill, he realised that if they were to stay here for anything more than a few days they would need to establish some sort of defensive structure. The few weapons they had were barely enough to stop even one determined zombie, let alone a hoard, or some mortals trying to take advantage of the situation.

Chapter 25

'How did society collapse so quickly,' was a thought that plagued Sam. One minute she was partying, the next there were scenes from every zombie flick ever shown; streets deserted, almost all aspects of civilisation in tatters. She wanted to talk it all over with someone, to try and understand it. and while Greg seemed the obvious choice, given her thoughts of him as a father figure, she knew he really had enough on his mind. He adopted an air of imperturbability, but she knew the private burdens he carried, as well as the responsibilities he had reluctantly taken as the de facto leader of the group. Smicker would try and make light of it, Seamus would give a military overview but no real insight beyond that. Tom, she was sure, perhaps had more perspective, given that he was a serving police officer.

When she completed her watch, she checked in some of the children' and answered another set of interminable questions from wee Billy she spotted Tom reading a night-time story to some of the younger ones. She waited until he finished and ambled up to him as he walked towards one of the camp's quiet areas.

'Hey,' she said. He responded the same way.

'What's up Sam.'

'Just some stuff rolling around my head. Sort of wanted to talk it over with someone."

'You got smokes, beers and Bucky I'm yer man.'

Of course, she did, no serious conversation in the camp seemed to take place without some sort of oral lubrication; they all were resigned to it as a coping mechanism, or maybe just because they were living and dying in Northern Ireland.

They settled down in a lee of the shorter of the two mounds, illuminated by the fading light of evening and the slow twinkling of solar powered lights. She pulled a bottle from her rucksack, along with a couple of cans of lager. For his part, Tom produced a fat joint, but she gestured to indicate that it was a conversation that was okay half-cut but not stoned.

'It's something that's been bothering me since I woke up to the apocalypse,' Sam began. 'Go on bender, black out, wake up two days later and the world has ended as we knew it. How did it happen so quickly? I just can't figure it out. Literally three days earlier…'

'Aye, that's the mistake you are making right there,' Tom said. 'It didn't happen that suddenly, it was there but the higher-ups were trying to contain it, and some higher-ups tried to take advantage, but none of them thought to share what was happening.

'Four weeks before it really sprang an old friend, a detective inspector I trained under, threw a file in front of me, walked into the car park and shot himself in the mouth. Poor fucker didn't die right away. Apparently as he lay there he kept pointing at the gun and his head as they waited for an ambulance. Might sound a bit sick, but I'm glad he died before it arrived, that way he wasn't coming back.'

Tom took a long, deep swallow from his beer and lit a cigarette.

'Jesus, Tom that must have been a right kick in the balls for you.'

'That's one way of putting it. He'd given that same file to about 20 people. Some were daft enough to mention it to their senior officers. They were re-assigned, or to be more accurate, fucking disappeared. I kept mine to myself. Only read it two days later. Fuckin' eye opener!'

Sam looked at him. She always suspected there was more to Tom than the ruddy faced, slightly overweight and jolly persona. It wasn't just that he was a police officer that had probably drank too much – common enough in the profession – but he sometimes had a dark look in his eyes that wasn't so much about anger, but about emotions that in his past had burdened him and remained buried deep down. The way he was protective over the children, the way he was the casual butt of many of Smicker and Seamus' jokes but never took the bait, just laughed along. Fuck, she thought to herself, stop being the psych-dickhead-therapist, just take it in. She trusted him, that's why she asked him.

'Apparently they knew how bad it was going to be months before it really went tits up,' he continued. 'Even the fucking scientists killed themselves when they realised. Everyone at Porton Down topped themselves.

'Of course, the wankers in charge did fuck all. You know they say that the government says there is a Cobra meeting to assess x, y or z, and it all sounds very dramatic and dynamic well do you know what their Cobra stands for? Cabinet Office, Briefing Room A.

'It is just a fucking room, before they went all American and called it a Situation Room.

'And do you know what they decided in their wee situation room? Fuck all. Rang other governments, called up soldiers and reservists. They even briefed Sinn Féin, and the Republic of Ireland government and the EU.

'As for the army, the top brass wankers thought it was an ideal opportunity for creeping martial law after years of cuts. You heard about those parts of Belfast that were closed off to protect the rest of the population. They were experimenting, like they were doing across the country. They wanted to see how compliant people would be when faced with the undead. If they had even listened to half of what the dead scientists had said they would have closed all of these islands, same as our friends in Iceland did. Complete. Fucking. Mess.'

He had delivered, what was for him a lengthy, speech, without once lifting his head. Now he looked directly at Sam.

'So, I don't know what was the tipping point, I don't know why it went completely fucked in the space of two or three days, but everything that had not been done made it inevitable.

The recently dead, the bitten, no mass closure of public transport, no serious attempt to quarantine, no widespread road closures, no sensible leadership…

'And, now we are here, FUBAR – fucked up beyond all recognition. But still going for another day, maybe more.'

Sam reached across and gave Tom a fierce hug. He froze as if unfamiliar with the gesture before hugging her back. She felt his tears on her shoulder, and she dampened his with her sorrow too.

As they broke off, each lit a cigarette and drank.

'Look, we are where we are Tom,' Sam said. 'I know Smicker takes the piss out of my music and how I dress but there is one line from of my favourite songs that for me says it all: 'they left us alone in the maelstrom, as you can see, we're clearly alive'.

'We're still here, we're not lying down, and I promise no more inspirational shit if you promise to be by my side.'

'Sam, you don't need me to promise you that, and I know you'll help me look after the little ones. We're going to make it to Iceland, we're going to try and start anew, or even just survive. I do have one confession though.

Sam raised her eyebrows.

'I fucking hate the cold.'

Chapter 26

'Just where do you take a proper shit in a pandemic? I'm talking about the glorious time, book in hand and good, solid one slithers out your arse, and it's almost better than sex, that feeling that you, the bowl and your bowels are conjoined as one, delivering a turd round the U-bend.'

'Smicker, would you fuck up, do you have to be so crude,' replied Jenny, half-exasperated, half smiling.

'No,' said Smicker. 'It's a serious question. I've seen you all, I've done it myself, sneaked off, quick shit, wipe your arse with whatever is at hand, and dander back as if you hadn't a care in the world. That's not a proper dump.'

It was then Sam realised Smicker was trying to fish for those struggling, and those in denial. Sure, as usual it was framed as a joke – albeit at schoolboy level. The short time she had known him Sam knew there was more smarts and empathy behind his smile and crudity.

He wanted to know what all in their group was feeling about the situation not just breaking any awkward silences. Seamus was unusually quiet but was looking around their group. They were two miles outside the last of the villages they had been through and had been surprised at how much they had been able to scavenge. Clothes, food, beer, and even a few tents, but they had to abandon the cars after coming across too many broken down vehicles, too many fallen trees, and to be frank, everyone was wary. They had nearly walked into a mini horde of zombies. If it hadn't been for Ruth saying 'I hear something' they might have all been dead.

When she said that Seamus and Smicker tried pushing everyone back, before Jenny opened up from her AK 47. What seemed random fire picked out forms that fell, Smicker and Seamus joined in, their weapons barking out, before

Seamus yelled to keep the bursts small. "Don't waste bullets! Don't just blast away! Wait, wait!"

They stopped their fire. Everyone in the group that was armed had their guns raised.

'Shoot to hit the largest part, their torso, then we walk forward as one and shoot them in the head, one shot.'

He looked round, nodded. There were short bursts throughout the line, and at each struggling form someone shot the undead in the head. Not all hit first time – they were not soldiers, but they eventually executed them all. A total of 17 undead been 'killed' in the first salvoes, seven in the second, until no movement could be seen. It had taken just short of 10 minutes, but the emotional exertion had been immense.

And Sam realised that was what Smicker was fishing for with his daft question about bowel movements. She was pretty sure that was not a part of any psychology course. Maybe it should have been.

Later they were camped at a road junction. All around were verdant fields, one occupied by a flock of sheep, some obviously in ill-health through the lack of farmers or vets at hand. The rest of the fields basked in the summer sun, oblivious to the human drama and deaths.

'See those lambs, what are they, six, seven months old?' asked Jenny. 'If we had time, I'd love a lamb roast with all the trimmings, proper sit-down natter, with no risk of some fucking zombie deciding you were going to be their dinner.'

'I wonder would zombies smell cooking lamb,' said Jude. 'But anyway, lamb's a bit fatty for my taste. Prefer a good wee tuna salad with feta, a nice lemon dressing and flat bread.'

'Jesus fucking Christ Jude, you now find yourself appointed as the survivors' Masterchef champion,' announced Seamus.

Chapter 27

Of course, there some members of the Icelandic government who didn't want to believe Kirstin's explanation of the outbreak, even one who ignored the evidence of emails and videos. She knew that few knew there was a CIA station just outside Reykjavik, and only three in the cabinet, but she thought more suspected.

'We can debate this whole thing forever, but we need to plan,' she said. 'I called Copenhagen just before you all arrived. I intended to speak to their foreign affairs minister, or someone of that status. A military general answered. He said most of the government were either dead or in detention 'because of circumstances' and that we either surrender total control to the new military-based government, or we would be on our own. Oh, and he asked how many zombies we had identified 'for purposes of military census'. I told him to fuck off.

'Ladies and gentlemen if you think I was wrong, vote that way then I shall resign. I'm going to step outside for a cigarette, and maybe a strong drink.'

She pointed at her secretary and said, "she gets a vote too, she saw what I did".

Kirstin walked to her office and out on to then balcony. The Americans might have loved Brennivin, but she preferred Irish whiskey. Go figure she thought, adopting the Americanisms that had crept into the Icelandic version of English. The bottle was dangling from her arm. A weight that needed relieved. She found an old unwashed glass she had meant to clear away a day ago when the world hadn't seemed quite as dangerous. She poured herself a more than a generous measure.

A few weeks ago she was a prime minister, with a

comfortable majority, working with a collegiate cabinet. She had even invited two members of the opposition to join her when it came to debating and agreeing fisheries policy.

Now she was considering how to lead a country with no army, no air force, a few fishery protection vessels, a coast guard and fuck all else in the face of a global pandemic of the undead. She pushed her hand though her short hair, took another drink and stubbed out her cigarette. Time to face the cabinet.

As she went into the room, she was conscious of the smell of cigarettes and the odour of whiskey on her breath. She felt vulnerable, but in her heart she knew the entire country was vulnerable, despite it being isolated compared to most. They all turned as she entered, and she immediately felt her heart quicken. Any of the people in the room could lead, but an election ago meant that she had the burden. But would any single one of them back her, let alone the rest of the population when she put forward her thoughts.

'Ladies and gentlemen, I have a plan that I would like you to consider.'

Chapter 28

'But why are there no helicopters or planes in the air," asked Jenny three days before their planned departures. Greg thought it was a perceptive question and was about to answer before Seamus stepped in.

'That's a good question and it has a relatively simple answer. Despite what you see on TV you don't just have a couple of handsome guys or girls launch into the great blue yonder. Behind every plane or helicopter there is a team of mechanics and ground staff, not to mention the air controllers, air force liaison officers and many others.

'In the 21st Century we ended up with more and more complex aircraft, but they all still need refuelled, they all need their computers programmed and they all need regular maintenance, practically after every flight. If you have a large proportion – shit even a small number – infected, dead, or whatever among the ground crew then the aircraft don't fly.'

Smicker, of course, had to interject: 'So, Hollywood has been lying to us all these years about the air force! Bastards! I thought you lot could just call in the fly boys to bomb the bad uns and rescue the heroes. Well, fuck I never.'

Greg laughed, and he saw the smiles; the tension eased.

'Fair enough, Smicker, but Jenny, your question is a good one. It touches at what we can expect in coming years, and it is very relevant about when you get to Iceland. The norms, what we have come to expect, are changed, if not gone forever. Flights abroad, well they came to a virtual end with Covid-19 and were only coming back in full before this shit storm. Flights now will only ever resume when there are skilled people who can service and maintain the aircraft, otherwise the Icelandic government would be laying on a first class, all meals included flight, rather than a few fishing boats.

Jude raised his hand, as always slightly shy when he was about to speak.

'Err, I was an aircraft fitter and mechanic' he said. 'But I can only work on one type of engine, like.'

'Aren't they all pretty much the same?' asked Jenny.

Jude, sort of slumped, his lanky frame seeming to fold around itself.

'Aye, if you have the manuals, someone who can guide you, and if you have time to practice. Give me four or five years I'm sure I can work on any engine, but it's also about the hydraulics, the control surfaces, the....'

His voice tailed off and he folded his arms across his bent knees and seemed on the verge of tears.

Sam saw then that Jude was older than he appeared, despite his youthful features and lank frame. He had several times offered insights and made suggestions that few others thought of. She reckoned that after five years in Iceland he would be in charge of their geothermal energy production.

'We're all going to have to adapt,' she said. 'We're going to have to learn new ways, new skills and even new ways to relate to each other, and we can't avoid that. We can wish we could, but we can't. Hey, it's a brave new world.'

The conversation waxed and waned along similar lines, with Seamus and Greg explaining how things everyone took for granted had ended. Sam's mind wandered and she needed to step away.

As the rest chatted, she walked up to the summit of the ancient motte, intending to watch the sunset and have some peace and quiet, a joint and maybe a few swallows of beer.

As she walked she saw Ruth walking almost parallel to her. She raised her hand and the teenager seemed to scuttle towards her, as if she didn't want anyone else to notice them.

CHAPTER 29

'Ladies and gentlemen,' Kirstin began. 'We are pretty much fucked. Isolated and while we have no cases, thanks to the lessons we learned in 2020, we are vulnerable. Sure, we have a few people who can handle weapons. I'm not sure it would be nearly enough should the military of Denmark or any other country decide they wanted to come here and take over, bringing martial law or even infections.

'Our situation makes our island a tempting haven for many nations, or any organised group. I've already asked that no further flights are permitted to land, something I hope you will agree is necessary. If any plane does land, I have asked the Chief of Police to deploy officers authorised to use deadly force for anyone other than Icelandic citizens.

'Even they will be arrested for making an illegal landing and detained for two weeks – a suitable period for quarantine.'

She paused. Even as a seasoned public speaker this was harder than she thought it would be. She reached towards the whiskey glass but chose water instead.

'I propose we ask for help, not just from anyone. I propose we try and contact Ireland and Scotland. By my estimation, based mainly on hunches and some papers the CIA officers had on them, these are the areas where the military is not the strongest, and we can set up controlled quarantine areas, and hopefully try to get some people that can help us reinforce our island, ideally some with military experience that can train people.'

Of course, there was a lengthy debate, she expected nothing else. After three hours she suggested they adjourn, meet in the morning, and put their decision to the population. Besides, she needed a drink to calm herself down, and maybe blackout the images of the men she killed.

Chapter 30

Ruth looked around her several times as she approached Sam, as if fearful that her chatting to Sam would be regarded as suspicious.

"Everything okay?" Sam asked, but Ruth, before answering indicated the lee of one of the higher sides of the park. When out of sight, her thin shoulders slumped, as if she had been wound up like a teenage ball of angst for so long. She pushed her fingers through her hair, and then suddenly hugged Sam. Hugged her so unexpectedly that Sam almost fell before she returned it. Sam had not expected the hug, but as they held on for a few moments she understood that they needed the physical contact.

'Can we talk, and like you won't say anything to anyone else,' Ruth asked.

Ooops thought Sam that was a big ask.

'I'll tell you what Ruth, I will not tell anyone unless what you tell me needs you to be protected, or it risks the camp or heading to Ballycastle. Then I might need to speak, but if I need to, I will tell you first. Is that okay?'

Ruth stood stock still. Sam, touched her shoulder, sensing the slight flinch.

'Why don't we sit down?'

Ruth seemed to fold as she sat, as if the even the limited openness had exhausted her.

'Can I have a cigarette please,' was the first she spoke in a full minute. Sam hadn't seen the teen smoke before but given the circumstances she didn't think it was an issue of Ruth's age to deny her. On her first inhale there was a brief spasm of coughing, before she settled. Sam recalled her first smoke at around Ruth's age, and the head spin that accompanied it.

'There are a few things that may be a problem,' said Ruth.

'I suppose, well I suppose I should have told you this soon after we met you lot, but I'm bi-polar.

'I was diagnosed after going pretty daft during the Covid-19 thing. I don't think they'll let me into Iceland and I've run out of my drugs.'

Sam put her arm around her, and this time there was no flinch, but a feeling that this young girl had resigned herself to fate.

'First of all, what drugs were you using,' said Sam. 'And secondly you came to the right person, I did a module on bi-polar treatments in my degree, so maybe I can help.'

Ruth stared in a wide-eyed manner that suggested she did not quite believe her luck, like someone checking their winning lottery numbers for the third time.

'I'm on lithium and olanzapine, but I was pretty much off the lithium,' Ruth explained. ""m not so worried about the lithium but I ran out of the olanzapine yesterday.'

'Okay,' said Sam. 'Don't worry about that, I don't know whether you know it but there are two pharmacies nearby. We sort of made it look like they had been ransacked in case anyone was looking for opioids to blot out the shit, but they are pretty much intact. We can go out in a while and see what we can get. I think there are brand names for some of the olanzapine but they all begin with 'z' I think.

'More importantly have you had any talking therapy or identified triggers for swings.'

'I had a couple of sessions for sorta behaviour things, and before I met Julie I was so down; oh I was on the verge of killing myself, but she needed help, I needed someone to talk to, and I've been just running on adrenaline, but as I saw the tablets running out I began to, well I got worried that I was going to go down really quickly. I've sort of known what foods set me off, but I think that bit is just in my head…'

Sam interrupted. 'Okay, let's get things organised, I'll let someone know we're going for a check on the perimeter, get to the pharmacies, and you will go to Ballycastle, and to

Iceland, and I'll be there with you whenever you need. No-one else needs to know here or there unless we both agree. You can tell me the other thing bothering you as we walk.'

CHAPTER 31

On the penultimate night before departure Greg needed some time to himself. Not an easy proposition given the crowded nature of the area they were camped in. Something had been bothering for some time, and he couldn't quite put his finger on it, but he suspected a lot of things were in play in his mind, competing with each other for space and time.

He finally decided to walk up to the demolished streets to the rear of the motte. Of course, he had to have a chat with the two sentries on watch, persuade them he was safe to go outside the boundary, that he was armed, blah, blah, blah. He suspected that within half an hour they would have summoned Sam, Jenny, Smicker and Seamus.

But 30 minutes should be more than enough time to help figure things out.

A quick scan of the surroundings, avoiding the booby traps and he sat on a wall. The house behind the wall now rubble, criss-crossed with trip wires.

As he lit a cigarette, he once again struggled with what was bothering him, then he realised he was excited. Yes, he was still grieving his wife and children and hating himself for what he did. Yes, he was still bothered about the fact that he had become, reluctantly, their leader. Yes, he was annoyed that even the military in the survivors expected him to have solutions. Yes, he worried that too many would die. But he could not remember when he had been so excited. He was never cut out for being a soldier, but all the reading, all the research left him in a better place than he could have expected.

He had only once been on a firing range before he had to shoot his family, and only had to fire a few rounds since, when they had been confronted with a small number of zombies in an estate near their encampment, and a brief salvo when they came across another group when they headed into town for more supplies. The thought of having to head into a proper fight, to try and provide some sort of salvation for those escaping to Iceland was causing him to almost tremble. It was part of his personality he didn't know had existed. Gone was the soft-spoken teacher, gone was the socially awkward teen, gone was the loving husband and father. Now, whether he wanted to admit or not he was an ageing warrior, ready for the fight.

Smicker and Seamus had agreed with them that should they survive beyond Ballycastle they would try and re-group nearby and search for other survivors. That too excited him more than he ever expected it would have. Fuck, should that happen he might just call himself General Greg.

Trust No One

'People are not themselves
Trust No One
Who is not who they say they are'

Conjuring Fate

Part Two

Governing

CHAPTER 1

Colonel Frank Brady walked into the concrete bunker.

'Good to see you Frank, considering the circumstances,' said Field Marshall Cameron.

Yes, considering the circumstances it's good to see anyone who's not trying to eat me,' replied Brady.

Cameron invited him to sit and poured them both a stiff measure of Scotch.

'Well, this is a pretty fucked up world, even before the dead started walking the earth, he said.

Brady took a long swig from his Scotch, looked around the office. Not the grand office such men as Field Marshalls occupied in London, just a concrete box on the edge of Aldershot.

'Sir, we've seen it go down so quickly, but I honestly wasn't expecting an armoured personnel carrier to be sent to pick me up, just two weeks after my wife died. As you sure you must know she didn't become one of them, but I am wondering what the exact fuck I am doing here.'

'I should have offered you my condolences, but we all have lost so much. Sympathy and all that, but I need you here.'

'For exactly what? I'm 57, six months away from retirement, and been behind a desk pushing paper for the last six years. I'm hardly going to contribute much.' Despite it being a breach of all sorts of regulations and being in a senior officer's accommodation he lit a cigarette.

'That is exactly why I want you,' said Cameron, pointing at the cigarette packet indicating he would like one too. 'You don't give a fuck as long as the job gets done. Come on, had it not been for you we would have both been up shit creek in Afghanistan. You disobeyed an order, won the day, blah, blah. I got promoted and you were held back from promotion because they suspected but had no real evidence.'

'Ancient history. You apologised, we went our separate ways, I got my time playing at being the big man in the 16th Air Assault and was relatively happy piloting a desk after that and Sarah and I had the time to play a little golf.'

Cameron sighed. 'Well part of why I wanted you here was because of one of the papers you penned when you were behind that desk, you know the one about military options in the wake of Covid-19? Well, if the pen pushers and politicians had put the money for the right build up, we might have been able to contain this shit a little better than the chaos that is out there.

'Three days ago, I was called by the Secretary of Defence, you know that slack-jawed, Etonian waste of space. He informed me that most of the Cabinet was dead, the PM's attempt to stay holed up in Chequers failed when a swarm of zombies overcame his personal protection squad, and nothing had been heard since. He said that he was de facto PM and given he had not been able to contact any of the heads of services I was now promoted to OF-10, in charge and my orders were to establish martial law.

'Even got a conformation in writing. Then heard the weasel had hung himself. Long and short is I am now in charge of the country. Not something I ever imagined or wanted, but here it is.

'We have a chance to ride this out, from what the surviving scientists are saying it does not look like the dead are rising from their graves like some bad movie. Once the bodies of the reanimated continue with their natural decay the threat will dimmish over time. Until then we implement the parts of your plan that involve corralling civilians in holding camps, feeding them, and protecting them if we can."

Frank looked at him steadily, poured himself another Scotch from Cameron's bottle, lit a cigarette and said: 'You know I wrote that paper when I was drunk and on painkillers after a car crash. Barely remember half that year, let alone what I was writing.'

'Well, it is being implemented as we speak and I need you to be part of that,' said the Field Marshall. 'I could order you, but I'd rather that you just agreed to it. If you agree you will be deploying to Northern Ireland in the morning to take charge of implementing your plan there. Hey, could have been worse, it could have been Wales.'

All sorts of memories came flooding back about his first tour in Northern Ireland, a frightened young officer, wet behind the ears in charge of men for the first time with the last dying embers of the conflict in that godforsaken country still costing lives and maiming soldiers and civilians.

'Why not Scotland?'

'You do not want to go there," said Cameron. "Rosyth naval bases, nuclear submarines, one in dock, two still at sea. I have had deploy all sorts of special forces types, naval specialists, cordons, and, truth be told, I have had to sign orders for executions.

'Add into that I have to somehow make sure we can ping that fucking sub every fucking day so that they know there is still a command structure, not as if any fucker told me the nuclear codes, or else I might let them just fire them to relieve the tension.'

Brady saw the emotion his former brother in arms was holding back, a mixture between anger and grief, as well as the burden of responsibilities.

'Look I am on the verge of ordering a complete assault on Glasgow, but I don't know that we have the forces for it to succeed, so for now it is just confinement and maybe burn down portions of it.

'On top of that a frigate went missing from Scapa Flow, just fucking vanished. Believe me Northern Ireland is a better option.

The field marshal steadied himself.

'Look Northern Ireland may likely have to become a strategic base when this shit show ends. We may have a de facto united Ireland emerging as we look to recovery, but you know how the Orange men and the republicans will want to kill each other even while fucking zombies are trying to eat them.

'Once you have some measure of control it might be an idea to get surviving political types together, and if the unionists kick off about an all-island strategy remind them zombies don't do border checks.'

Brady lit himself another cigarette, and without waiting for Cameron, he poured himself a large measure of scotch. As he swirled it around his mouth, he mused that this was not an order he could refuse, if Cameron was already ordering executions, a tough move for a man usually a stickler for rules. But then again it was something Brady knew he had taught the old shit back in Afghanistan. A story never to be told.

'Okay, seems like I have no option,' he said. 'What are the exact orders?'

Cameron poured himself a measure, looked down at his desk, picked up a piece of paper, and threw it on the ground.

'One of the last serviceable chinooks we have will fly you and a team of officers and senior NCOs to just outside Carrickfergus tomorrow. You will establish command post, take charge of whatever or whoever is there. The chinook will load up with barrel bombs and hit every part of Belfast it can until it runs out of fuel, or crashes. Anyone refuses they are to be executed on the spot. Ideally, I'd napalm the whole fucking city and create a dead space to work in, but we don't have the ordinance or the aircrew to maintain planes, seems like the pandemic killed off all our engineers…'

He trailed off.

'Can I have another one of those ciggies Frank,' he finally said. 'Fuck. I could have never imagined me in charge of the country, ordering executions, ordering whole cities to be burnt, but I can't think of any way to keep us going until this all…well this all blows over.

'Oh, and by the way I'm giving you a field promotion to

full general. If we survive, you'll get a better pension if the banks ever return. You'll need someone to keep the soldiers paybooks up to date – you know how some of the other ranks want to think they'll get beer money.'

Chapter 2

The next morning Brady was standing in a new set of combat DPM's. He thought – a fat load of good would the latest disruptive pattern material do. He recalled a line from the old film about the Second World War assault on Arnhem. As the parachute force advanced one officer remarked that they appeared to be wearing the wrong sort of camouflage for urban warfare. He wondered whether the attempt to secure Northern Ireland would be another Bridge Too Far.

The chinook was powering up as his new XO, Major Simon Carragher approached. He had asked Cameron about Carragher being young looking for a major. The Field Marshall explained in short brief sentences: 'Lieutenant at 20, captain a year later. Applied and accepted into SAS. Fought and led in some of the more clandestine special forces little fire fights.

'Returned to his regiment after a disagreement with some of the older members, promoted to major after one wise old colonel spotted men obeyed his orders better than any other, even if it meant keeping him off the frontlines.'

Brady looked him straight in the eye. He was his own deep resolve reflected there.

'You're a bit of a hard bastard, aren't you," he said as a challenge to Carragher'

'And I hear you are the same sir.'

'Yes. And I want everyone on that helicopter to understand that, and everyone we assemble in Ulster to understand the same. The time for niceties is long past, we are to consider this a war zone in which we fight a series of battles. Of course, it is not really, but everyone has to have that attitude. We can only fight for ourselves and whoever is prepared to obey martial law.'

As they watched their squad of six helping ground crew load barrel bombs the major provided some welcome news.

'We have made contact with Palace Barracks command,'' he said. 'Two Para were stationed there for some familiarisation with other members of 16 Air Assault. They lost a shit load but they and members of 2RIR and a reconnaissance platoon have made it out of there and are holed up in the hills. We have ordered them to report to Carrickfergus. In total we expect there to be 100 we can call upon.'

Brady recognised that was more than indeed welcome news. He had worked with, and been part of, the brigade before and knew that there was a quiet professionalism behind the tough reputation. He also knew they were the type of soldiers to obey orders and fight through to achieve them.

The Chinook crew indicated that they were ready, and Brady filed in behind Carragher, looked at his squad, the barrel bombs and took his seat. The pilot looked back, Brady gave him the thumbs up, and the double-bladed beast took to the air.

Absent-mindedly he passed his fingers over the new general's insignia on his shoulders, the crossed baton and swords. He had no idea how Carragher had found one on the base, but he suspected the major was adept at finding a lot of things others couldn't.

Chapter 3

The chopper lowered to a height just 100ft above the waves as they approached a field a mile outside Carrick. He had decided the PSNI station near their landing was to be their command post in the first instance as there were already a group of soldiers gathered there as indicated by earlier comms.

As soon as the ramp lowered the squad made a well-rehearsed exit, covering all angles with raised rifles as a soldier emerged to welcome them.

Brady hung back. He needed to speak to the Chinook crew.

"You know your orders, and you will carry them out," he said. "You may have qualms that there will be civilian casualties, as you have been told, but consider that you are probably saving them from being infected.

'I also know that you are not sure with the load and the time needed to drop the barrels that you will be low on fuel and probably not be able to make it back to the mainland. If so, please return here, we will need every able-bodied person.'

The pilot looked round at his crew. 'Thank you, sir.'

Brady walked around the helicopter and saw that Carragher was about to introduce him to their liaison.

'General Brady, this is Colonel O'Neill of 1RIR. He has been in charge of Sea Park to date.'

'Colonel, as you know I have been put in charge, but until I am fully briefed please feel free to continue as you are. Major, get your squad billeted, and report to me in half an hour. Colonel, can you join him and bring a summary of the intel to date.

'Oh, and I don't suppose you could find some Irish whiskey for the briefing?'

He mused on what they had seen from the air, the fires, the roads clogged with abandoned vehicles, and a sense that like the rest of the world that this was the end of times.

He looked across Belfast Lough and saw the first of the barrel bombs explode and quashed the qualms in his mind. He still had his orders.

CHAPTER 4

Colonel O'Neill had managed to find a bottle of Bushmills and a bottle of Jameson's from somewhere, and Brady indicated they should enjoy a glass before the briefing.

'Thank you, colonel. We all need this before we go on,' he said, taking a deep swallow. 'Now you can begin with a brief round-up of where we are.'

'Before I do so sir, I want you to know that I am not a full-timer, just a member of the TA who got promoted after I stopped being in the regulars. Been merely a pen pusher, keeping some sort of order in the weekend soldiers. I was a manager in a human resources company before this all happened.'

'Well, that might be exactly the sort of skills we will need Colonel,' said Brady. 'We have a lot of nervous troops, and they may need occasional man management skills and more diplomacy than I will ever have.'

Carragher looked Brady up and down. The slight onset of jowls framed a slim mouth that had few laughter lines around it. There was a small paunch, but the squared off shoulders and the hint of muscles kept in shape told of a man who wanted to stay fit. He knew of his car crash, and that he had been steering a desk recently. But he had more battle experience than many and was known as a ruthless bastard, to enemy and allies alike. Even with those who he was in direct command of. Not exactly a diplomat indeed.

'Perhaps you can begin Colonel,' said Brady, looking for signs of nerves or fear.

'Well sir first of all the remnants of 16 Air Assault will be here before nightfall according to their last communication at 11 hundred hour. There is a total of 115 of them. They are travelling cross country, and they have two land rovers that they filled with rifles, machine guns and ammunition, as well as two light mortars. We are not exactly blessed with sufficient arms, so this will be needed.'

Brady mentally noted that O'Neill referred to them as rifles, not as SA80s or the official term of LA85 IW. Maybe he had been away from the regulars too long, Maybe, he was just forgetful. He was a slim man, features pinched, receding hairline and wearing delicate designer glasses. Carragher would soon find him some administrative tasks to keep him out of the way.

'What about the surrounding area?'

'Sir, we have established a perimeter around the base that extends to about one mile, we have sufficient to maintain that perimeter, but little to do any offensive tasks. We have been monitoring civilian movements, and as requested we have been urging them towards Carrickfergus and the leisure centre.

'The PSNI have been escorting them there and trying to keep them secure. They are mainly using surviving officers from response teams so they are used to some extent familiar with crowd control.

'As to the castle…'

Brady had noted the ancient Norman Castle on his briefing back in England, stout stone walls that had withstood the test of centuries, access to the harbour, and easy to set up a surrounding screen.

'…some civilians are holed up there. Drone footage shows there to be around 40 people there. They've closed the gate, but from what we can see they are largely unarmed and do not appear to have much in the way of provisions.

'The northern approaches to Carrick, both from inland and along the coastal road have been secured by PSNI and some of the local TA. Part of an arch on the coast road has been demolished, but in such a way we can easily clear it with some explosives, if needed.'

Before he could go any further Carragher interrupted: 'It is the suburbs that concerns me, there are entire estates there, and we have no idea how many people are either dead or re-animated as the undead. Have you completed any recon?'

It was a good question, one that had been nagging Brady. Carrick and its castle presented an opportunity to establish a good foothold, and, if all went to hell, easy access to the sea and a boat to anywhere but there still was a sufficient number of houses close that could harbour too many undead.

'We have a Royal Marine who is an expert in explosives. He was here on leave but volunteered to assist. Don't know his full background, but he seems to be from one of the Marines special units.

'He rustled up what little plastique explosives we had and used it with fertiliser to flatten much of the estates. Still a few to do, but so far we've created a number of impenetrable zones.'

Carragher doubted there was anything truly impenetrable in any urban or suburban areas. He glanced at Brady as the general looked at his watch.

"Gentlemen, it is now 15:30," he said. "I'd like to have some time to absorb this. Colonel can you pull together any written materials and any further electronic materials for me to look at. Also, I'd like a full manifest of all under your command at present, to see if there are any men I recognise or know of. The local police commander, or whoever is in charge, will need to meet me too.

'I suggest we reconvene at 18:00. By then some of the assault brigade should have arrived and settled in. Their most senior officer will join us.'

O'Neill stood, saluted and left the room. Carragher was about to join him when Brady motioned for him to say.

'What do you think?'

'Well, sir, not sure how he survived as a regular or how long he would survive as a colonel in a full-time front regiment. But he seems to be doing what he can with the resources and infrastructure he has.

'We will need to relegate him to administrative duties because I don't think he has the balls to be in a straight up fight, nor does he have the ability to make a strategic assessment, just makes tactical decisions.'

Brady looked straight at his XO. The man stood at an impressive 6 feet six inches but had a lithe look about his frame; one that could move quickly and without hesitation, despite the deceptive hunch he put on at times.

'The slight ruddiness in his cheeks, he hoped, was a natural feature and not as a result of the bottle. But then again, he supposed every man, woman – and here in Northern Ireland probably every child too – had been indulging to fill up on all the Dutch Courage they could muster to simply keep going. He took a mental note to cut his own whiskey consumption right down. Well, after tonight, because he believed that it was all going to go very wrong unless he got a handle on the situation.

CHAPTER 5

The stragglers from 16 Air Assault had arrived just 15 minutes after their scheduled time. Brady had observed them coming in and noted the calm efficiency with which they unloaded and made safe their weapons despite evident weariness in their faces.

The briefing with O'Neill, Carragher and the captain from Two Para, who gloried in the name of Smythe-Talbot. Both he and Carragher took an instant dislike to him. As Brady poured a slug of Bushmills into his morning coffee he reflected that he did not need to be a mind reader to note that dislike in Carragher's demeanour. Christ, the Captain was everything that had destroyed the British Army for too many years; officers straight out of some private school Army Cadet shithouse, university then Sandhurst and an automatic sense of entitlement without earning respect or trust. Too many NCOs had sacrificed their lives keeping little people like him alive over the years. The sergeant in the squad of the six he flew in with knew more about fighting and leading than this twat ever did. He wondered how he had ended up in 16 Air, but presumed it was a familial thing, either in the forces or through some political clout somewhere. He hoped that the rest of 16 Air would ignore anything that this slack-jawed excuse for a human ordered.

Then O'Neill completely silenced all present.

'Of course, we need to discuss what we do with our captive zombies.'

Brady looked at the bottle of bush wondering was either he or O'Neill totally wasted. He finally gathered some semblance of his own sanity in this asylum.

'What the fuck do you mean by captive zombies?' he shouted. 'There were explicit orders to eliminate any fucking zombie near any fucking bases or command post. As in eliminate it meant eliminate, not make them your new undead friends.'

O'Neill's face reddened and he pushed his glasses up.

'Sir, those orders also allowed for capture and containment, if it can be safely done for, a, experimentation or b, to use as a method of intimidation for recalcitrant civilians.'

Smythe-Talbot opined in studiously cultured tones: 'Well this could be awkward.'

Carragher ignored the captain.

'Firstly, have you been ignoring the elimination order, secondly how did you capture them, and thirdly, where are you keeping them.'

Brady admired that direct, simple set of questions, each could be easily answered by a competent officer, and equally they could contain traps for anyone too cocky for their own good.

O'Neill explained this, like the good human resources manager he had been before the crap hit the wall, in sentences that sounded as if he was reading off a carefully prepared PowerPoint presentation. The various members of various regiments had coalesced around the police base as per orders. They had secured the armoury at another barracks seven miles south. In returning to Sea Park they had continued the implementation of Operation Crusade orders and had killed every zombie in their path.

Rifles had proved effective, but not everyone had a good enough aim to guarantee a head shot. Police had begun the risky but effective tactic of using a baton to club the undead in the head before delivering the coup de grace with a single round from their pistol. Some had even used tasers to subdue them first.

'It was very effective, we only lost one soldier out of the 75 that had embarked on that operation, but we had the problem that the bodies were accumulating at various choke points,' he said. 'We had to burn them. Some of those who had been on that expedition were a little, shall we say shell shocked upon our return, and truth be told I was a little shaky as I'm sure you are aware I should not have led that jaunt myself.'

'As to your second question Major, it came about by accident. Those that had been overly spooked by the experience were set to manual duties. Sergeant Allen suggested they be set to digging trenches deep enough that the limited mobility of the zombies would mean they could not easily get out and could equally be easy to dispatch.

'With about 400 yards completed in the fields to the north west a private reported back to myself and Sergeant Allen that there were three zombies stuck in the deepest part of the trench and what should he do.

'Of, course he should have killed them right away, but he and his fellow entrenchers were only armed with one pistol between them lest their shell shock got the better of them.

'When we arrived, with a platoon, there were, by then, six zombies struggling and flailing against the mud. Sergeant Allen shot the one that seemed the most lively in the forehead from 20 yards. Quite a shot.

'Before he trained his weapon on another one, I ordered him to ceasefire remembering the caveats to Operation Crusade.'

Carragher asked again where they were being held, and with a sense that there may yet be potential in O'Neill given how they had detained the undead.

'There is a car park area that was being refurbished before the pandemic. The fencing had been 90 per cent completed and was reinforced to quite high standards. The fact that part of this facility was also a forensic laboratory made it seemed opportune to capture a few should experimentation be required or use them like rabid dogs to intimidate.

'As to how we captured them, the men came up with a simple enough solution, rope them as if lassoing a horse. Three ropes were usually enough, but they were strong beyond their wasted frames. We then simply dragged them along to the car park, face first, arse first, sideways. They didn't seem to mind.'

Brady mulled this over and asked, 'How many do you have?' When the colonel replied there were 17 Brady responded: 'Gentlemen, I shall have to consult with the command at Aldershot on this. Get yourself something to eat, and captain see if you can organise me a fresh cup of coffee. We shall reconvene in 20 minutes.'

Chapter 6

He had no intention of talking about the captive zombies with the Field Marshall. He more than likely end up on the line with some staff officer who was likely harassed and in reality only able to pass the message on. They should be eliminated immediately but he thought that he did not want to burst O'Neill's bubble too soon. He would need that local knowledge, and despite his first impressions the colonel seemed to have good organisational skills. Given how few he had under his command Brady was astute enough to know he needed that. Would be worth pairing him up with Carragher. Together they would complement each other. As to the zombies, to be considered later.

As he mused a knock came. The man introduced himself as Sergeant Allen, the man with the good shot according to O'Neill. He put a plate of food in front of Brady.

'Everyone else was eating sir, thought you could do with a bite,' he said.

'Sit down Sergeant and join me.' He poured the man a whiskey and sipped his own as he pushed the mash and sausages around his plate.

'Bit of a shit show Sergeant," he grumbled as much at himself as anything else. 'How long have you been in?'

'Almost 15 years. Ten in the 2RIR and five in the signals. Only had a year or so to go before going into civvie life, sir, but well, as you say, the shitshow happened.'

Brady supposed the man was in his late 30s but looked like he had aged a lot in recent days. He must have been a once fit man, but he looked to have put on a lot around the middle. However, like every good NCO he had served with, his eyes still had the alertness, and no doubt those lips could command ranks to obey fucking orders and do it fucking immediately. At a guess Allen had done several tours in the godforsaken lands various governments had decided to sacrifice ordinary soldier's lives.

His hair was shaven to an almost severe standard, his face clean and slightly reddened, heightened by a nose that looked to have been broken a few times. His lips were almost protruding above a long prominent chin. To Brady he looked to have features that had been put together by a child, but he suspected that was because of his combat experiences, good and bad.

'Going to the signals would have been a good move in normal times,' Brady said, offering the Sergeant a cigarette. 'Could have nabbed a good civilian job.'

'That was the plan, sir, telecoms sort of thing.'

'Allen, we're about to have a briefing of sorts, lots of officers with lots of different opinions and some with self-importance beyond their years. I'd like you to sit in and listen. Don't go and say anything as some will never listen to the common sense of a sergeant. Tomorrow I'd like to hear your opinion. Not so much about what they suggest, but how they say it. Understood?'

'Yes sir, as long as you know I won't beat around the bush when I say it.'

'I would expect no less. Now tell the serried ranks of officers and wankers to join me in five minutes. Oh, and compliments to the chef,' he said pushing the untouched plate away.

CHAPTER 7

The briefing really didn't tell him anything he couldn't have garnered with a few interviews, but he needed the officers to start thinking like a staff HQ. He did know that from the dispositions, locations of other 'outposts', and the number of active services that they were woefully short of weapons and ammunition and had next to none in terms of larger munitions and transport. Six armoured police Land Rovers, two soft skinned Land Rovers and little else that could be reached.

After the meeting he asked Carragher to begin assessing how and when they could acquire more if they could. The major had already been thinking about this and suggested a few options, none of which were easy.

The next day Allen was prompt in reporting to Brady, even before the general took his first sip of coffee.

'Well sergeant, your thoughts?'

'As I said, permission to speak freely?' When Brady nodded Allen began.

'As a rule 60% or so of officers are useless at seeing both tactical and strategical objectives. In this case there seems to be an even higher percentage of uselessness.

'Colonel O'Neill isn't bad for a weekend soldier, but he can only see in the immediate, not long term. Good at speaking to the ranks without coming across as a pompous git.

'Your XO, Carragher is obviously a bit of a hard case. I'm guessing he's had time in special forces. Good at asking the right questions at the right time, but he maybe needs to lighten up a little in front of the regulars and part-timers as he could come across as aloof and that doesn't read well. Nor will it do so when he is dealing with the police.

'Captain Smythe-Talbot should not have ever been allowed

to wear a uniform. Sir, best described as a twat. Not sure if he has ever been in combat, but I am pretty confident that the guys in 16 Air would not follow a single one of his orders in combat. In a firefight he might, as the Americans would put, get fragged. I am also not sure what impact he would have if kept away from the front and based here as there would be discontent within hours.'

Allen gave a few more summaries and observations on others that had been present before adding.

'As to yourself, you think you've been handed the shit end of the stick, but with nothing else to do at the end of the world you are all in and will not hesitate to take the hard decisions.'

Fuck me, thought Brady this man is very astute.

'By the way sir I studied psychology at university before getting into a little trouble with the law and joined up after serving three years behind bars. That was in the days when you didn't need to be squeaky clean to join."

'Thank you, sergeant, that was very useful. Now how would you feel about a field promotion?'

'No thank you sir. I'm perfectly content. I may have had a good education and all that shit, but over the last 15 years I've learned to love the soldiery and leading by example. I couldn't bear ending up in the rear echelons, and having to pore over maps, orders of battle, sending this here and that there. Just tell me what you want to achieve, and I'll lead the men and women to the best of my abilities.'

As he finished his sentence two shots echoed around Sea Park. Allen was at the door seconds before Brady who was instantly flanked by two of the men who arrived in Northern Ireland with him.

'What is it?' Allen ran ahead to where he saw men congregating. Shouting them to move their arses out of the way he saw two men just outside the main building's rear entrance. Both had gunshot wounds to their heads. No coming back.

A lance corporal turned and said he saw them aim for each other quite calmly, nod and each shot the other one.

Brady looked over the scene. 'Chicken shit suicide pact then.'

One man's aim hadn't quite as clean, or he had been hit just a little late. Rather than the clean shot in the middle of the forehead the top of his skull had been ripped off.

There was a tiny moan from the blood-soaked mouth. Allen drew a pistol and loosed a single round into the lips bubbling with death's froth.

'He was gonna die anyway and we'll not be doing palliative care here.' He looked around the ranks, not at the officers. 'No palliative care, got it? You get wounded, too bad. You better find a way to go yourself as I won't be wasting any rounds on ya.'

Carragher arrived as Allen was making his mini speech. He glanced at Brady, who nodded.

'What the sergeant said may not sit well with you, but remember this, if you are injured is it better to put one in your own skull than have a fucking zombie eat you alive? That should be incentive enough not to get injured.'

Chapter 8

Brady was watching drone footage when a knock came to the door and O'Neill and Allen stepped through. He gestured them to sit.

'Sir, you asked for a full round-up of the other locations where we have troops, and a summary of the PSNI forces.'

'I do recall Colonel, just leave it on my desk, but both of you look like the cat got your tongue, what's up?'

They looked at each other, but before they could speak Brady put a bottle of Jamesons on the table and urged each to drink 'to loosen their tongues'.

'First up there's a PSNI inspector out there, very pissed off that she wasn't invited to meet you as, in her words, they had been doing the dirty work for the soldiers. And, Sergeant Allen has had an idea on how we can use the zombies, if needed.'

'I'll deal with the inspector momentarily, but I'd like to hear what your idea is sergeant?'

'Well sir, it occurred to me that while we have the zombies confined and controlled for now we may, at some time, the need to use them. I was on leave, sort of, in Japan. The police there use a type of sasumata…'

'A fucking orange sergeant?'

'No sir, it was developed in the 16th Century, basically as a long stick with a hook or long spiked bar for Samurai to arrest common criminals in a non-lethal manner. Modern versions are in use by Japanese police to contain potentially violent suspects, or those on drugs.

'Basically, it is a long stick, with a rounded end. Push it against the neck or chest and you can direct the criminal to where you want them to be."

'Might be useful if some of the bods want to study the

zombies or corral them.'

Brady mused for only a few seconds: 'There's bound to be some REME about, or some territorials that can rustle one or two up, if needed.'

He wasn't about to admit that a plan was coming to mind on how to use the zombies.

'Now please be so kind as to invite the inspector in.'

Inspector Barbara Samantha Bryson bundled past O'Neill, marched right up to the very edge of Brady's desk, threw her cap on it and stared directly into his eyes. Brady took a moment to assess the gaze, the woman's hair, tightly drawn into a short ponytail, her face an almost perfect V shape from her eyes to her chin, and fury pouring from every pore.

He stood up and extended his hand. She looked down at it as if he was holding a diseased bird but took it and shook it briefly.

'You are fucking lucky I've calmed down,' she began, before Brady interrupted.

'First of all, I'd like to apologise for not asking to meet you earlier. It's an old army habit to organise briefings amongst themselves without involving others and making too many assumptions about what others are doing, but please be assured that it will not happen again, if you so wish.'

Inspector Bryson, finally sat down, lit a cigarette, exhaled and said: 'How long you been preparing that wee speech?'

'Well, it has been used quite a few times over my career, usually after a fuck up or three, but I am genuinely sorry. In the briefings I received since I arrived the police role in the surrounding areas was explained, but I put it in a mental file and never really considered that you and your colleagues have been bearing quite a load.

'I intend to lighten that load and involve you in our planning going forward.'

Bryson set her unfinished cigarette in the ashtray, looked down at it before fixing the general in her gaze.

'Look, thing is this is pretty fucked up, and I've been left as the most senior officer anyone can find, I'm just a fucking inspector. Yeah, I led tactical support groups, but not any other command. Luckily the ones I knew rallied around and we have exactly 150 officers, of which only half are fighting fit, most of the rest are too tired to be useful or have been injured.

'And the civilians are less than happy to be told where to go and where not to go right now.'

Brady raised his hand briefly, poured her a stiff measure of whiskey, and lit a cigarette of his own.

As he exhaled, he looked at the tiredness in the woman's eyes, and the simmering resentment she had been containing.

'Right, I am going to allocate 50 of our air assault soldiers to rotate them in on a 48-hour basis to allow you to rotate the same number of your officers for some relief, until we can organise further. I will be having a senior staff briefing tomorrow to firm up the planning. I'd like you to be there, with an experienced sergeant who isn't afraid to provide input. For now, would you join me in having something to eat?'

''Thanks, but no thanks, I need to get back to see how things are at the leisure centre, but I will be there tomorrow. But before I go, don't fuck me over general, because I will take my own action if you do. Good day.'

She stood, turned, and did not afford any acknowledgement as she left the room. Brady mused that such an officer would have been an asset in any of the conflicts he had the misfortune to be sent to throughout his career. Only his late wife Sarah had exhibited such verve.

CHAPTER 9

The briefing was close to a disaster. Smythe-Talbot stuck his useless ideas in at every opportunity, and every soldier present and the two PSNI representatives looked uncomfortable each time his jaw swung open. He had not mentioned it to Brady but instead waited until everyone was present to say he was not happy to have to release 50 soldiers to relieve police. He had received his orders that previous day and picked those to go forward, and not a word was said. Now he said 'highly-trained assault soldiers should not be on policing duties'.

Brady was about to explode, but he saw the expressions on the others. Carragher eyes were staring into the mid-distance, but it was clear they were ready to snap back, no matter what was being said. Allen was looking down at the table-top with an intensity that threatened to bore through it. Even O'Neill looked ready to go full on ballistic.

But it was Bryson who ended the captain's vocal shitstorm.

'Would ye fuck up, you are one daft cunt if you can't see the fuckin' ballix we are in. Stuff you're fuckin' Sandhurst shite up yer arse and get with the survival programme here. When you grow some hairs on yer balls you can offer an opinion.'

Brady stifled a laugh, Smythe-Talbot looked as if swallowing wasps would have been preferable, Carragher looked away, barely concealing his contempt for the captain as well as his admiration for the police inspector.

'Right, we've enough going on without more arguments,' said Brady when he composed himself. 'Captain, please speak to me after the briefing. Now I need details about the situation in and around the castle, the mood of the civilians and intelligence on any groups of civilians in a 20-mile radius.'

For nearly an hour various information was bandied about

the room, some useful to the general, some not, but he was beginning to get his priorities in order. He would need some time with Carragher and possibly the sergeant and Inspector Bryson to sort it all into an actionable plan. The briefing fizzled out and all were moving away. Smythe-Talbot looked to have forgotten the request to stay behind and was moving towards the door.

'Captain, please sit,' Brady said, barely concealing a growing anger he had squashed while the briefing was going on.

'If you ever try to undermine my orders like that again I'll bust you down to private and have you personally flogged. I. Am. Not. Fucking. Joking.'

'But sir I was…'

'You shut your mouth for now. If you had a concern about your orders the proper course was to raise it with myself, or the major. That is the chain of command. I don't know how you learned military discipline, or who gave you such an entitled fucking attitude, but you will listen to orders, you will note them down, you will raise any concerns in an appropriate way.

'Oh, and by the way I served as part of 16 Air Assault, and those men know the boundaries of when they are supporting local police in theatres of operations, and they know when they are in the fight with local forces.

'Now get out of my sight and if you see the inspector apologise to her, call it a misunderstanding if you must, but we need the police to make things work, if it actually works out at all.

'When you are done with that, organise a reconnaissance party to search for petrol or diesel for the generators tomorrow morning. Don't fuck it up.'

Smythe-Talbot slithered away, leaving Brady with his head in his hands as soon as the door closed. Sighing he raised his head to scan the pile of papers and maps, poured himself a large whiskey and lit a cigarette. He was coming to realise that even holding out for a month was going to be a challenge.

There were too many variables, too many elements to consider and the knowledge that he had too few resources. What worried him most was any groups of civilians that had holed themselves up. Once they got past the survival stage they might go onto a defensive posture and there would be no shortage of weapons at hand in Northern Ireland should they not want to fall under military control.

Chapter 10

The next day Brady was ruminating about how time was slipping. He had heard worrying reports from Carragher that civilians were becoming more restive being camped behind barbed wire and feeling corralled by armed police and soldiers, even when it was explained that barbed wire was an effective barrier against zombies.

Sergeant Allen had become his de facto aide-de-camp as well as a useful sounding board amidst the mayhem. He could see him just outside, smoking away, chatting to a couple of paras. When he turned Brady gestured him to come in.

'Sergeant, can you access the drone footage, and if the inspector is available ask her to join me, as well as the major.'

Just a matter of minutes later they sat down, and Allen had the drone footage from around the castle and leisure centre on screen.

'As you can see those inside are beginning to signal about food, and as you know the populace is becoming restless at the leisure centre. We can't keep them this way, without utilising them in some way that they feel useful,' Brady began. 'What I propose is that we ask for volunteers to help fortify the town at key positions – always accompanied by police or troops.

'That way they can be invested in what we are doing here. Thoughts?'

The inspector looked down before speaking: 'It's a sound plan, but some of the so-called civilians have 'links' with paramilitaries and may take the opportunity to re-visit where they have stored weapons or drugs. That would be a dangerous mix.'

'Agreed, but they are the ones likely to be stirring the shit. Make them think they are important but keep an eye on them.

Inspector could you or other officers identify those that, as you say, have links to paramilitaries? If so, you could have some troops accompany them to make sure they keep their proverbial noses clean and away from any white substances that they may want to put up those same noses?'

Before Bryson could answer Carragher intervened.

'I'm sure that the inspector could pick out those to keep in control, however, I would be concerned that there will be those that could pose a problem without us knowing it and may agitate. There are, as I understand from the inspector's briefing, one or two minor politicians, who, no doubt, as soon as the shock wears off, will want to have some sort of say.'

'What do you suggest?'

'Well, ask them to take on a role – not much really – to organise a rota, a watch system, plan meals, and the like.

'Would keep them occupied and play to their self-importance. And they no doubt also have an awareness of who the paramilitaries are, and, without asking them to grass them up, they could act as eyes and ears, sort of thing politicians seem to like.'

Brady nodded: 'In the meantime, I'd like to get my own eyes on the situation. Tomorrow, Inspector, would you accompany me on a trip through the area. Major, I'd like you and Sergeant Allen to ride along in another vehicle with drone overwatch.'

Chapter 11

Hindsight is a wonderful thing, thought Brady, but that decision and the ones he made in subsequent days may have accelerated the disaster.

CHAPTER 12

As soon as they approached where the civilians were encamped Brady's shoulders tensed. Yes, they were being held but with access to food, shelter, and sanitation but the rolls of barbed wire and patrolling soldiers and police made it look like a prison camp. He turned to Bryson and she met his gaze with her usual intensity.

'It is the best we could do,' she said. 'I know what it looks like and if there was another way I don't know. Most accept that the barbed wire and armed people is necessary not to keep them in but any wandering zombies out.

'I do fear that having such a large group of people could attract a horde, but if dispersed they are more likely to be picked off or behave even more stupidly.'

'We really need to think this over,' Brady replied. 'You are right, they represent a tasty banquet for any of our undead friends that might wander by.

'Are there any similar areas that we could divide them around?'

'There might be a few but having enough of us to guard them will be the challenge,' she said. "Do you want to see them?'

He nodded and radioed Carragher to follow them and keep the drone ahead.

They took a u-turn and headed back towards the coast and the castle. Their driver slowed as he navigated past a burnt-out car and a single round hit the armoured windscreen and bounced off. Before he could finish saying fuck Carragher, Allen and the three paras with them were out of the vehicle and delivering rounds in a furious fusillade. Brady bundled himself out of the back, staying in cover.

"Ceasefie, ceasefire, fucking stop now!" He yelled as the inspector came to his side, her Heckler and Koch at ready. He noticed she still had the safety on, but her thumb was ready to flick it.

'Fuck sake Carragher, those are solid walls, it would take artillery to bring them down. Back to your vehicle all of you, pull back a couple of hundred of yards and put the drone up.

'So much for the fuckers being unarmed.'

Although Carragher and Allen went back to their vehicle he noted that the paras walked beside it as it reversed, weapons trained at the castle.

He and Bryson climbed back in. He ordered the driver to back off who only replied: 'As long as you don't mind me smoking, near shit myself there.'

Brady could understand that. The round had stellated a small bit of the windscreen, and had it not been armoured the driver's head would have been right in line.

'What's your name officer,' he enquired softly. 'That will be 'rad sir, Brad Gibney.'

He was wearing the familiar PSNI 'riot gear' and despite the bulk it gave him he had a thin face with darting eyes and a receding hairline. Brady guessed that this was one police officer who would have been more content giving out speeding tickets than policing the apocalypse. He reached his own packet of cigarettes to Gibney, who at least managed to keep his hands from shaking.

He ordered Allen to bring the drone monitor to his vehicle but kept the choice words he would have for the major and sergeant for later.

Bryson leant forward to say something to Gibney, who seemed to be beginning to get his heart rate down.

Brady's own was pounding, he resented poor discipline, understood how it could happen, but expected NCOs and officers to set an example, not open up without assessing the situation. This wasn't Afghanistan's rag heads, then he checked that thought, realising that it was both racist and wildly inappropriate to even think it.

A rap came to the rear doors and Allen peaked his head in first, muttering an apology.

"That's for later," Brady said. "What do we see from the drone?"

Allen turned the small screen to the general: "As soon as the drone appeared they all disappeared apart from this guy."

On screen there was a tall man, long hair pulled into a ponytail, with his coat on a parapet, and a rifle resting on it. He was certain that it was a Lee Enfield of late Second World War vintage, but Brady knew that in the hands of someone who could hit a moving vehicle from that range it was someone who could hit anything he wanted when in range.

On screen he watched as he pointed in the direction of the drone, then cupped his ears towards the land rovers. He repeated this, an apparent invitation to parley.

CHAPTER 13

'Look at the graffiti,' Brady said.

'Yes, seen it a few times,' replied the inspector.

Spray painted on several walls out of Carrick and in Eden was 'Kannibal Killing Krew'.

'It bothers me, not just that there seems to be some self-appointed group, but the initials. KKK. Last thing we need is some right-wing nutjobs with survivalist leanings, weapons and they might not be the most able militarily but I'm sure they can still be dangerous.'

They had been driving, leaving the castle situation to be handled by Carragher, towards the power station. Brady had taken O'Neill's assessment that it would be difficult to see how it could be re-started but wanted to see if there was anyway. He hoped, some of the civilians corralled in Carrick had some experience.

He realised it was, probably a vain hope, but despite the calm demeanour he was trying to keep up in the face of facts he was beginning to grasp at straws to establish how he could move forward to make the country viable and controllable in the next few months.

'Don't suppose you have any intel on this group Inspector?'

She shook her head, just as Constable Gibney slowed the Land Rover and muttered: 'might be a wee situation ahead.'

Ahead were four shambolic figures, zombies straight out of central casting, ragged clothes, greying peeling skin, vacant eyes, walking down the middle of the road. A fifth was pulling itself along the pavement on its elbows, its legs missing. Behind them was what appeared to be a child's body that had been ripped into bits. Brady noted that the hand of the child was dangling from one of the walking dead's mouths. Even though he had seen some horrors in his service he felt bile rising. He was thankful Bryson ordered the second land rover to flank theirs. On command three soldiers and two police officers dismounted. Brady ordered controlled salvoes only.

The stillness of the day was then filled by staccato fire. Aiming at 200 yards wasn't accurate, for even the best drilled soldier, but Brady noted that the five walked forward steadily, firing deliberately. The first rounds knocked the zombies backward, their remaining guts spilling behind them. A pause and a few controlled bursts. Finally, within five yards the coup de gras, double shots to the heads. It was over in less than 30 seconds. The general was pleased how they had performed but wondered how even the best drilled units would perform against a horde, or a civilian uprising.

The three men and two women walked back to the land rovers, the soldiers' weapons sweeping the houses, the police officers alert to the road ahead.

A corporal twirled his left hand in a gesture, and all returned to their land rover, and they moved forward, the heavy vehicles' wheels crushing what was left of the undead.

There was no need for conversation, just a glance at the inspector, who still had a steely expression, no emotion evident.

'There's the power station entrance ahead,' said Gibney.

Brady ordered the halt to the vehicles, and for the first time since arriving in Northern Ireland, donned his helmet, not to show his fear, but an indication to those around to take shit seriously. He was glad he did.

They were surveying the surroundings, noting the fence and the two mutilated bodies around it when the first rounds rang out. The corporal who had taken charge of their escort just a few minutes earlier was shot in the neck. More shots came and Brady felt shrapnel ping off his helmet. The men and women took cover behind the land rovers. The vehicles were peppered.

Brady counted the rounds and tried to estimate the

direction. When there was a brief pause, he gestured to the crouching soldiers and police. Four fingers, four shooters, spread out at the hedge.

A private nodded and let a short burst of fire back before another plucked a grenade from his webbing. He showed it to all, before arming it. Brady indicated with all 10 fingers, and the man nodded – throw it in 10 seconds.

The lobbed grenade was followed by a lance corporal opening up with his light support weapon. As they did the inspector was already moving round the opposite flank firing short bursts from her Heckler and Koch.

Brady was doing pretty much the same from his weapon, but he watched too as hardened members of 16 Air Assault followed Bryson's example. There was some desultory response that ended almost as soon as they had opened up on the hedgerow. One soldier advanced towards it, backed up by a colleague advanced in a half crouch. Four shots. Brady knew the four shooters had been dispatched without mercy, whether wounded or not.

As ever the firefight was over in seconds and he knew, he like the others, would be high on adrenaline before the shakes kicked in.

CHAPTER 14

They returned to Sea Park, with the corporal's body in a body bag, only stopping near the castle to give his decision on what to do with those inside. Short, and no doubt influenced by the encounter at the village. 'Tell them if they throw out the rifle they get ration packs. They don't throw out the rifle, they starve. Either way they have 72 hours to vacate the castle.'

It was a subdued party that settled back into Sea Park, not just the death, but the fact that the power station seemed out of bounds, unless they went into it with significant force, which Brady knew was not possible at this time, without risking multiple casualties.

He settled into his office and was about to pour himself a whiskey, when a rap came to his door, Colonel O'Neill. He gestured him to sit down.

'Sir, I fear I have some news that might not brighten your day,' he said.

'Well spit out, no time for shit talk right now.'

He poured two tumblers of Bushmills, passed one to the colonel, before lighting up a cigarette.

O'Neill seemed to consider how to explain, pushed his glasses up, straightened his back.

'It's the reconnaissance patrol led by the captain, I'm afraid they took casualties and the captain himself was injured. There were two fatalities.'

Shit, Brady thought a half competent idiot like Smythe-Talbot couldn't fuck up a simple recon mission, especially as he must have known the need to sustain the generators.

'They are expected to be back shortly. From what I can gather to date they were attacked first by several zombies, which they repelled. They then parked up at a petrol station when they were fired upon by several people. An NCO made the report to me, a Sergeant Robbins.'

'Okay, send this Robbins into me as soon as they return. Ask Major Carragher and Sergeant Allen to come in. Please join me when Sergeant Robbins can join us.'

O'Neill left and Brady managed to keep an almost silent 'fuck' out rather than explode, as he felt right about to fly into what he knew could be a dangerous rage. He drained the whiskey, noted O'Neill hadn't touched his tumbler, pulled it back to himself and finished it in one swallow. He considered another one but held back.

When Carragher and Allen came in he had composed himself but needed to get something clear first.

'Sit. That display while we were at the castle. You are two experienced soldiers you should set an example. I can understand covering fire, but to open up at random, thereby encouraging those under your command, was immature and not in line with the doctrine you were both trained in. I will let it slide for now, but understand this very clearly, I will personally make sure your cheeks and ass will be red and you'll be busted down to doing night sentries. We must conserve ammunition, we must set an example of calm professionalism, even when we are all shit scared. Understand?'

They both nodded and were about to issue muted apologies when O'Neill and Sergeant Robbins came in.

Robbins was a squat bulldozer of a man, his five feet eight frame bustled with muscles, he had bright blue eyes above a nose that was almost bulbous. He drew himself to the ranks before him and struck a stiff salute. His uniform had blood splatters across it, and his left hand was covered in a bloody bandage.

'Sit down, and take a moment,' Brady said. 'Would you like a shot?' gesturing towards the whiskey.

'No thank you sir, don't touch the stuff, only beer. I would, however, like a cigarette.'

Brady tossed the packet across the desk. 'Sergeant Allen,

do you think there are any beers around?'

'I managed to acquire some that might be hidden at various parts. I think I can rustle up one or six.'

He exited and once again Brady watched Robbins closely. Someone who joined up at a young age, he guessed and displayed leadership skills and had gradually ended up in the paras as the sort of rugged improvisational man who could take charge. Brady urged him to think of how he could describe the recon patrol.

In an improbable short time Allen returned with 12 cans of lager.

'Sorry, they're not cold, but the Colonel ordered only food in fridges and to turn off fridges not in use.'

'Wise move,' said Brady. 'Sergeant Robbins, can you please tell us what exactly happened?'

Robbins described Smythe-Talbot assembling a 20-man team, a mixture of air assault and locals, to depart in three land rovers and proceed towards Belfast, to assess where there might be petrol stations along two arterial roads.

CHAPTER 15

Smythe-Talbot was poring over a map in the lead land rover. He was still smarting over being balled out and making his half-assed apology to that bitch of an inspector, knowing that his upper middle-class tones had her almost wrinkling her nose in disgust as he spoke

More importantly he knew that the men and women would have heard some way though Chinese whispers about him being cut down in verbal flames. The only way he could reassure himself that it would be okay was to demonstrate to that old fuck, and those that he would have to command in the days ahead he could do the job.

They were pulling out of a roundabout, when his driver indicated ahead. There were about 30 zombies ahead, shambling about, but beginning to turn towards the sound of the engines. He thought briefly about ordering a team to open up but thought that it would be a waste of ammunition.

"Drive on through them," he urged, and a corporal relayed that to the other two land rovers. They revved their engines and soon there was the bumps of bodies being crushed beneath the tyres.

He asked one of the local RIR men, where the nearest petrol station was, and he said it was next right, two hundred yards ahead. He also warned that it was on the edge of a large housing estate, with a significant paramilitary presence before the world collapsed.

Smythe-Talbot considered it briefly before deciding that he should not show any reluctance.

'We'll press on.'

He ordered a land rover to cover the road northwards, and another along where they had come from, while he parked up beside the garage. As he stepped out the crushed remains of at least two zombies were mashed into the tread of the land rover's tyres. He thought that he better make sure that was hosed off before going back to base, lest Brady be given another excuse to rip into him.

Four men formed a perimeter, while another two began the laborious task of lifting the heavy covers and beginning to siphon what was there into jerry cans. There wasn't much, just three gallons of petrol and a gallon of diesel. He was considering asking if there were any more filling stations nearby when the corporal in the northerly land rover reported that there was a small supermarket and an off licence relatively untouched. Given the old man's liking for a drink, he thought he might earn some redemption.

CHAPTER 16

'And, sir, I advised him not to, and he said they had enough cover with the land rover to the south of us, which he ordered to come up within 100 yards,' said Robbins. 'As soon as we got close to the supermarket, I advised that this was perfect for an ambush. He said there was enough cover and firepower not to worry.'

Brady and Carragher exchanged looks. Carragher mouthed the words 'mission creep'. Brady nodded and turned to Robbins, gesturing him to open another can of beer.

'As soon as we arrived the others in forward land rover had already dismounted. A few were lighting cigarettes, and some were noticeably edging towards the off licence.

'I was beginning to post a few men as a screen when the other land rover arrived, and the captain was ordering a sweep of the supermarket and off licence. As he walked towards the off licence there was the first salvo. That's when the captain took the rounds. I returned fire to try to suppress, but as the combat medic got to the captain, he took two to the legs. He was bleeding out and with the incoming fire no-one was in a position to get to him.

'That's not an excuse sir. I know from Helmand that you can end up being the next one.'

'No need to apologise sergeant, I did my stints in that shithole and no-one wants a posthumous medal. Carry on.'

'Must have been one of the local reservists with us, because we had no heavy machine guns when we left Palace, but he opened up with the gimpy from the top of the rover. Ballsy thing to do, but he laid down enough for us to get some semblance of how we could organise a defence. I went to the medic, but he was gone. I grabbed the captain by his collar and pulled him back. That's when I realised he wasn't wearing any ballistic armour.'

'What!' exploded Carragher. 'Who the fuck does he think he is, too posh for rules.'

'Calm down major, he's paying for it,' said Brady. 'Colonel, can you issue an order that no one leaves here without full kit, oh and make sure to advise the inspector to make the same provision for the police.'

Robbins tale hadn't much else. Those that were firing upon them had set up the ambush pretty smart, with two enfilading firing positions, but after the initial bursts it had been clear that they were not expert shots.

With the RIR man giving cover from the general purpose machine gun, they were able to establish a screen and manoeuvre the land rovers to establish shooting positions. They concentrated on the fire from the hedges opposite the supermarket, and when the fire from that direction eased they drove one of the land rovers straight into the rest, 50 yards south of the supermarket, and, 'battlefield justice was administered'.

Chapter 17

On the first evening when they arrived from England Brady had watched Belfast ablaze, the barrel bombs having set enough of the city alight to spread. The iconic cranes of the shipyard silhouetted in flames that seemed to be licking the very sky. There wasn't much of a cordon sanitaire around the city, but it would have to do. As long as the roads towards Carrick were blocked and manned as much as possible it would have to suffice for now.

He totalled in his head the forces he had under his theoretical command. Maybe 200 soldiers here in Carrick, another 70 or so in Derry, as well as the police. Not nearly enough. He pondered the possibility of recruiting some civilians to help the policing tasks, but the thought of arming some current or former paramilitaries gave him the shudders.

Sergeant Allen knocked, and with a gesture he ushered him in.

'Sir, I thought you would like an update on the condition of the captain,' he said. 'I'm afraid it's not good news.'

The hardened part of Brady's soul whispered that they would be better off without Smythe-Talbot, and any further waste of medical supplies. He nodded to Allen.

'It appears that he won't last the night. He's drifting in and out of consciousness, but he asked to see you.'

For a few moments he pondered refusing this last request but then thought about how some would see that – the optics as the politicians would say. Would be bad form as the word would get out that as well as being a hard ass he didn't care about anyone under his command. In fact, he thought he should have done it earlier.

When he arrived in the side room the captain it was obvious the man was on his last legs. The round he had taken to the scalp was superficial, but the gut shot was enough to tell him that infection, damage to his intestines and probably a few other bits of the stomach being shredded was enough to spill shit around his bloodstream. Walking towards the bedside he thought he was too late, but saw the slow, laboured rise and fall of the captain's chest. When his shadow crossed the captain's face the man's eyes flickered open. His left eye was filled with blood and his nose, usually thrust forward like a caricature of the upper-class inbreeding looked to have sunk into his cheeks. As he opened his mouth a small bubble of blood tarnished his lips, and a grotesque image of a male prostitute he had beaten up when he was a teenager came to Brady's mind, and as he pushed that regrettable moment in his life aside just as Smythe-Talbot spoke.

'General, I'm so glad you came,' he said, each word punctuated by a rasping breath. 'Wanted to apologise for everything.'

'No need captain, no need.'

'Yes, sir there is. I tried to undermine you, and I fucked up a simple patrol. Truth is I didn't want to be a soldier. Was daddy's idea. Wanted to be a banker or lawyer but was a bit too thick for that.'

He paused, this time each breath slower.

'Always thought if it came down to seeing actual combat, I'd get shot in the back from one of the other ranks...'

With one last heave of the chest he passed. Brady reached out and closed his eyes, noting that the wound in his stomach was an exit wound. That didn't mean anything, but then again in the circumstances there would be no enquiry.

Chapter 18

Just before the disastrous day had started Brady had taken what he assumed was a final briefing from Cameron's chief of staff, a bland piece of shit, all peppered with the usual, hold firm, blah de fucking blah.

But now Carragher was gesturing him out of the dead captain's room, a sense of urgency in his eyes. Once they were alone, he whispered, 'Field Marshall himself will be on the blower in 15 minutes, full battle code, ears only type of thing.'

'Well fuck that, I want you there too, fuck the old man.'

Within five minutes they were set up in the office, a glass of whiskey in front of each of them, Brady chain smoking, Carragher trying to ignore the fug billowing around the room. Probably never smoked, thought the general, when his musing was cut short by the bleat of the radio.

The message was short and not so sweet, punctuated by Cameron's reassurances that they would only have to hold on about nine or 10 months as the undead were decaying daily and there were no reports of any rising from the grave.

'Well, fuck me sir, that's a new level to the clusterfuck.'

'Yes, major, a clusterfuck, How the fuck are we going to take on a frigate and an organised civilian militia backed by fucking Iceland?'

Cameron's message informed them they had finally tracked down the missing frigate, it had been commandeered by the crew, some SBS 'types' and was now under the titular command of the Icelandic government. It was set to rendezvous with a 'crowd' from north Antrim and the Field Marshall considered this as an affront to his authority, but also as important was to need to set boundaries to ensure the future 'status' of the UK.

'Any suggestions Major?'

'Sir, we don't have the numbers or expertise to achieve anything other than containment, nor do we have the type of weapons to hand that could threaten, let alone take on a frigate. Type 42 I presume.'

'I don't give a fuck what type it is, there is no way I will expose what we have here to shore bombardment, or generally getting screwed over.'

Carragher sat looking at the general. A few days ago, he seemed indominable, confident and sure of himself. Was it the deaths in the past 24 hours that had him looking so weary or was laterally realising the enormity of the task he was faced with just to keep some semblance of order, never mind protecting civilians and maintaining the rule of law. However, as the general lit another cigarette, he recalled Brady had been in the shit storms of Iraq and Afghanistan and had been on one of the last flights out, memorably thrusting a cigarette up a Taliban commander's nose before giving him a lighter. There was a photograph of that incident in a few barracks up and down the country, usually captioned with something racist. He was entitled to look weary after his service.

Chapter 19

When his wife died, Brady had been floored. It had come so suddenly. The day before they had been talking about driving down to their cottage in Cornwall, riding out whatever the fuck was happening. But when went to get up the next morning, Sarah, grasped his arm, looked into his eyes and whispered in a rasp: 'I think I'm having a heart attack'. Then the grip tightened until he felt her nails dig into his flesh and then slacken. Her eyes were open, but there was no life. He had moved her onto the floor and tried CPR until his shoulders cramped, all the while knowing it was futile. He slumped at the bedside and gave one last kiss to the woman who had been with him through the best and worst of times, who calmed him down after the shitshow in Afghanistan, who persuaded him to see out the last years of his service behind a desk, after the car crash.

In the kitchen he touched his own lips, the memory of kissing a mouth that was now already cooling. He resolved to bury her here in the garden she had tended whether he was abroad or at home. He didn't know if she would rise again like the fucking zombies, but he would be at hand if she did.

That afternoon he wrapped her in two bed sheets, and with effort he dragged his wife into the garden. He was in reasonable shape for someone his age, with the golf he and Sarah both enjoyed completing his rehabilitation after the crash, but after the first six inches of soil he was out-of-breath. Cigarettes, no doubt. He sat on the edge and lit a cigarette. As he was drawing his first puff he heard a voice.

'Uncle Frank? You okay?'

It was his nephew, Jordan, offspring of his useless brother and slightly less than useless sister-in-law. Still, by some miracle Jordan had turned out to be half-intelligent, holding down a job in investment banking, or something.

'Is that Aunt Sarah,' he said pointing at the bed sheets.

"Yes, heart attack. What about Bill and Penny?'

'Can't find them. Came back from London last weekend when things started getting hairy. Had to pay some of the cops a fortune to let me out of the city, but the house was empty. Only came out as I'm nearly out of canned food, beer and cigarettes.'

Brady threw him his packet and motioned towards the house. 'There are a couple of bottles of scotch in the kitchen and there should be beers in the fridge.'

As he waited for Jordan he finished his cigarette, tossed it on the lawn and thought that if Sarah was a ghost now she would be tutting and telling him how lazy he was. It brought a small smile and a brief, small, sense of levity to his grieving mind.

Jordan came to his, side, two glasses, two bottles or scotch and two beers balanced on a tray Brady couldn't remember ever having. They toasted each other and Sarah. For a few minutes there was only distant birdsong before Jordan asked if had been digging a grave.

'Yes. I don't know what the fuck is going on with these zombies, whether they would eat the dead, or Sarah will rise as one, but I'm not taking any chances.'

'Do you want me to help?'

'To be honest that would be really appreciated. There's another spade in the shed.'

For the next hour they worked in tandem, only taking a break for a cigarette and drinks. They had managed to get down to about four feet when Brady noticed Jordan had stopped. He looked up expecting this weed of a man to be looking another break. Instead, he saw the shovel in the grave and Jordan's eyes blank. Drool dibbled from purple lips. He reached pallid palms out to Brady.

'Jordan?'

From the drool-soaked mouth came a low moan.

'Jordan, stop fucking about!'

He took a stumbling step backwards as Jordan came towards him. He scrambled out of the hole, grabbed his shovel and with all his strength he swung it at Jordan's head. It connected clean, cutting deep into his head. As Jordan fell, Brady pulled it out with some effort and swung again, this time the flat of the shovel stoving the face into a pulp. He hit three more times, even though he knew he had killed whatever Jordan had become on the first blow.

Brady shovelled a few bits of dirt over the body, then he looked at Sarah's wrapped body. He wasn't going to dig another grave – or to be honest with himself, he couldn't. He shuffled over to where Sarah's body lay, and dragged her over and tipped her in. One of her arms had slipped through the blankets. He lifted his shovel and began to fill in the grave, musing that she liked Jordan, so…

It took him nearly three hours to fill the grave. When he was done, he sat down and gulped deeply on the bottle of scotch. He thought the next day he would cover the grave with stones.

Eight days later the APC arrived, and he had only just stopped crying.

CHAPTER 20

Carragher wasn't sure about his orders to carry out recon on the north Antrim group, especially after the chaos in Carrick. At least with Sergeant Robbins accompanying him he was assured of an experienced man at his side.

He spent the day planning routes and going over the scant details from the briefing. They still had no detailed drone coverage of Ballymena, and every time a drone came close it just stopped working, and Brady wasn't going to risk any further attempts.

Robbins was poring over the map, when they heard the commotion followed by a volley of shots and a several rounds of pistol fire.

They looked at each other, confusion writ large. Confused or not they responded, picking up weapons and running to the sound, Carragher just about beating the sergeant through the door. Outside was a scene of milling soldiers and police, two bodies in the middle of the crowd, and Brady screaming at Allen and a private Carragher didn't recognise. One of the men that had accompanied him on the flight to Carrick was pushing the crowd away, barking out orders to move, to get back, to carry out orders and the usual 'nothing more to see' much beloved in the army.

Brady turned to Carragher and Robbins, gave them a gesture to come closer.

'You can stow your rifles, these two aren't going anywhere,' he said. 'As for him, I'm not so sure what the fuck I am going to do yet.'

A man in a rag tag uniform top without insignia and wearing jeans was standing to the side of the bodies, initially hidden from view by the crowd. He had Lee Enfield rifle trained on one of the local territorials and had a look that suggested he had done more than his fair share of fighting with bare fists.

It was then that Carragher recognised one of the bodies as Colonel O'Neill. He had not recognised him at first, given that half his face was blown away, the right side of his jaw dangling on to his collar. The other body had two wounds in the chest, and another had shattered most of the back of the skull.

As he was glanced up at Brady he heard Bryson.

'Jesus fucking Christ, what the fuck happened here,' she said. Brady replied, asking her, Carragher, and Robbins to meet him in his office. As they walked away Carragher heard the General tell Allen, in a whisper that had all cliched sound of a threat: 'second fuck up Sergeant. I'll give you the benefit of the doubt this time, but next time you are out'.

As Carragher walked with Robbins he noted that Bryson had unclipped the strap above her pistol. She must have done it when she had heard the shots but had the sense not to draw it until she was closer. Mentally he noted that she had more professionalism about her as well as a determination few could match amongst those in the base.

At the door Brady told Allen to make sure the prisoner was secure and 'clean up that fucking mess'. Before he was even seated Bryson was pouring herself a generous measure of whiskey, not waiting for any bullshit etiquette about senior officers and all that. The General didn't seem to notice or care. He just poured one for himself into a mug and half-heartedly gestured with the bottle to the rest.

As he lit his cigarette Carragher asked him what had happened.

'A cluster fuck. Two deserters, one dead and a dead colonel. And it was a fucking civilian who caught the deserters, not one of our assigned patrols or sentries.

'To cut a long, useless, fucking story short, two of our so-called soldiers decided that they didn't like the way things were shaping out and wanted to make a break to the marina and borrow a boat to go who knows where. This civilian was coming to tell us that the locals were getting restless, and some had gotten hold of guns and drugs. He himself was someone you fired on, guy in the castle. Apparently, the Lee Enfield wasn't the only weapon he had, and he escorted him to the perimeter, where he insisted on staying until a 'ranking officer' came; goes by the name 'Knifer'. O'Neill and Allen went and were escorting them here.

"They had just arrived when one of the would-be deserters grabbed O'Neill's sidearm and shot him. Allen shot him before he could do anything else. Oh, before you all look at me like I'm making this up I'm surmising from what I heard from the shouting, what Allen said before you arrived and what I am guessing, but it adds up. Carragher, when we finish here, quick questioning to find out if I missed anything.

Inspector, can you check in with your officers to find out if the claims hold any water. Robbins, check out our perimeter and the sentry duties. I don't want any more surprises. And passwords for anyone approaching the perimeter, from inside or out. No passwords, they are to be arrested. It may be the end of the world, but we need to retain some sort of discipline."

His cigarette had burned down to the filter by the time he had finished and as he lit another one Carragher noticed for the first time how the task was weighing heavy in him. From what he had been briefed before joining him, Brady had lost his wife shortly before the shit really hit the storm and had been a few months from retirement before being scooped up by the CIC to take over here. Part of him sympathised with the 57-year-old, part of him thought the field marshal had picked the wrong man. This wasn't Iraq or Afghanistan. This was an operation that required someone who could think clearly, not lose his temper. That could be expected, but should be controlled, especially in front of all ranks and civilians. Brady was showing the signs of his temperament becoming all the more ragged.

Sure, drinking all you want was fine when piloting a desk,

smoking as much as you want, and reminiscing about the good old days when you could shoot ragheads and sand niggers, as the Amercans and other ranks called them, but it was not useful here and now. He didn't know exactly what had happened on Brady's last tour in Afghanistan, but he knew it was bad, brutal shit that left a trail of bodies, and not all of them Taliban.

CHAPTER 21

As they left Brady swirled the whiskey around his mug. He finished it off with a deep draw that seared the back of his throat. He stubbed out his cigarette and his fingers stroked the handle of the pistol on his hip.

'Oh, so fucking easy to just put a round in my head and join Sarah,' he mused. 'I could just do it and jump into the blackness.'

The thought was only with him for the briefest of moments, but that Black Dog had haunted him before, and he knew it could come again at any time. PTSD, depression, anxiety, there wasn't a serving man or woman who left their regiment after combat who didn't suffer in some way; the price they paid for doing their duty.

But, right now, despite what Cameron had assured him of the undead eventually dying off, he knew that he may not be able to survive much longer. If the cigarettes, booze, and dodgy heart didn't kill him, then one of the men out there might put a round in his head anyway.

In the meantime, he had to shape what was left of this rag tag piece of shit that he had been handed into something that at least stood a chance of surviving and may be even obeying those orders to reach Ballycastle. But he needed some sleep. Just three hours was not going to do in the coming days, especially when it was sleep brought on by whiskey. Looking wistfully at the bottle he decided he had enough for today. Calling on the sentry at his door, he said he was not to be disturbed and lay down on the bunk behind his desk. Sleep was elusive at first, but when it came there were dreams of Afghanistan, of Iraq, of O'Neill's body, of the many other bodies he had seen – and caused. In the dream they were not the mangled lumps of body parts but wore a deathly pallor and sounded the groans of the undead.

And they were all coming towards him.

Waking with a start Brady almost screamed. He glanced at his watch. It was time to get his and others shit together.

Speaking with a cigarette clamped between his lips, he ordered Allen to gather up senior NCOs, senior police and bring them. The nightmare lingered, but with it had come a plan, for good or ill.

As they sat down, with only a little conversation mumbling around, Brady called them to order.

'I have orders, that I am not entirely comfortable with, but they are nevertheless orders. Inspector Bryson, these orders do not apply to you or any PSNI officer. You can decide if my plan to fulfil those orders is appropriate and you wish to join in what I propose.

'I have been ordered to prevent an evacuation of civilians from Ballycastle and re-take a stolen Royal Navy frigate. And, yes, that is correct, re-take a frigate.

'To complete both these tasks is as close to impossible, while at the same time affording some sort of protection to the civilians we have in and around the town.

'Major Carragher, you and Robbins are to proceed immediately to complete your mission. There is a Land Rover fuelled and ready, and a driver on hand. The less you know the better. Radio only when you have established some firm information.'

The two exited the room, almost slowly, Carragher unsure compared to his normally easy gait.

As they left Brady resumed, as before in terse, clipped tones. For all the fuck ups and general chaos, this is when he felt comfortable, in command and with a clear plan to work on.

'I intend, tomorrow, to proceed to the town, establish if any of the civilians have experience in seafaring, then liberate one of the boats in the marina to take us to Ballycastle. Another group will proceed along the coast road towards

Ballycastle. Before going there, we will rendezvous at Larne for the final briefing. Another group will remain here to provide some sort of cordon and protection for the civilians. If, as I have been led to believe the infected will begin to die off in coming months, then we will need some sort of population to remain healthy. Any questions?'

The group glanced around before Bryson spoke: 'I know the road to Larne and beyond. I was stationed there as a rookie. I don't believe you should have your rendezvous there, it's chaotic at the best of times, but I suggest that a few miles up at Carnlough or Glenarm would be a better option. And, if you wish I could lead whatever group you want to send down that road.'

'Very good, I will organise that"' the general replied.

"I believe that at least half my officers would feel safer closer to home, and in charge of the town and the civilians. It's what they know best, rather than being an attack force. From what I gather the situation when they arrive is not one best suited to the regular constables.'

The conversation ebbed and eventually flowed as the details began to come together about how many would be in each group timings and what armaments they would need. Brady began to relax for the first time since he was picked up by the APC. He was also buoyed by the amazing discovery by one of the corporals of a LAW 80 anti-tank weapon. There might be a fighting chance of at least stopping or delaying the frigate, if not seizing it.

CHAPTER 22

Carragher suspected the mission was going to be a fuck up when he met their driver, Private Patterson. His pinched face suggested he would rather be safe at base, but he had the air about him of a wannabe boy racer, even complete with driving gloves and his sleeves rolled up as his hand rested on the gearstick. Perhaps he should have reminded him it was a Land Rover he was driving not a pocket rocket modified hatchback.

For the first half hour of the journey had Carragher telling him several times to ease up as he braked late into corners, accelerated too much at every opportunity. He could hear Robbins tumbling about and swearing in the back. He swerved around every abandoned car as if it was a chicane on an F1 circuit. As they passed Antrim Carragher saw three cars across the road. He was about to tell him to stop but before the words formed Patterson swerved onto the verge sending the Land Rover on to two wheels and then on to its side, metal crunching and Carragher thankful he had worn his helmet. As a matter of long habit, he checked himself over. Patterson looked dazed, blood coming from his nose where it had collided with the steering wheel. Carragher's side of the vehicle was pinned against the verge. Unclipping his seatbelt he pushed towards Patterson, trying to get the man to respond and climb out. He slapped the private twice in frustration, before the man pulled himself towards the door: he hadn't even been wearing a seat belt.

When he pulled himself and the dazed driver from the vehicle, he shuffled them both towards the back and pulled the door open. Robbins was dead. No helmet, head trauma from one of the weapon cases. His skull had been popped open, one eye dangled from its socket and his lower jaw was a shattered mess. He heard Patterson throw up behind him. He didn't care whether it was shock from the crash or seeing the sergeant's face, and he didn't care. Grabbing extra magazines, a spare rifle and grenades from one of the broken weapons cases he turned, fully intending to assess Patterson's state he heard a low moaning to his side.

It came from one of the cars, and he could see a grey, almost skeletal figure clawing at the closed window. He remembered from the early days dealing with the pandemic that those moans would only draw more of the undead. And he suspected that there may be others, still quite lively nearby. The three cars seemed arranged and there was too little damage to the bodywork for a collision.

'Patterson, pull yourself together, we may have company coming.' No response. He looked over the private's shoulder to see what he was staring at. Four of the undead where pulling themselves out through hedges. The lead one, looked sturdier than the rest, but still grey skin and tattered clothes and that slightly unsteady walk.

'Patterson, your weapon, use it.'

Before the soldier could respond Carragher knocked off the safety of his rifle. The four zombies where about 40 metres away. He slowed his breathing for two seconds and fired. The first zombie's head took the round square in the nose and fell forward. Shifting his aim, the next two went down in a similar flop, then from almost at his ear the blast of a dozen automatic rounds. Patterson was blazing wildly. It would be okay on the battlefield in covering fire, but it was useless here. Turning slightly, he pushed Patterson's rifle down and whispered, stop. The fourth round he fired was as efficient as his others.

He took a second to gather his thoughts. From the crash to his firing had lasted less than a minute and a half. He knew that he did not have the option to allow the adrenaline to fade.

'Right Patterson, we need to get the fuck out of here double-quick fucking time. Check if one of those cars can drive and I'll try and salvage some of the equipment from the rover. Do it! Now!'

With some netting he pulled cases, a light-support weapon and a gimpy free of the back as he heard an engine rev. Patterson had managed to start a BMW M5. He stood out of the car and shouted.

'Sir, they left the keys in the ignition, and there's almost a full tank.'

"A bit convenient Private."

On the last syllable a voice came from out of the field to his left.

'Hope you don't think that you're gonna steal our car, now, are ye?'

A broad Ulster accent, sounded like a Belfast one. The man was dressed in a faux combat jacket and tracksuit bottoms. He looked about six feet, srawny, with a white bandana tied around his forehead; the letters KKK written in black. Behind him were three others, with a similar lack of sartorial lack of elegance, all with the KKK bandana.

'Just what I fucking need, vigilantes', he thought to himself.'

Patterson already had his hands raised, reaching upwards as if trying to touch the sky. The major was trying to assess how much shit they were in. The man who had spoken held an AKM towards the major, two of the others held pistols, while the fourth had a baseball bat. Carragher's rifle was on his shoulder, no chance to pull it off and fire. Rather than address the vigilantes Carragher chose to shout at Patterson.

'Private put your fucking arms down.'

The four, briefly glanced at Patterson. It was enough for him to release his pistol. He still wouldn't draw it. The man who had spoken could let off a full clip before he could draw and aim.

'Well, well, well, what have we got here, wee soldier heroes. Fucking could have been one of you cunts before I wised up. Still, proper snared you heroes with our wee roadblock, but I'm pretty impressed with the way you took out the zombies.

We had them tied up waiting for wandering souls to draw them away from what they were driving.'

A rambler, thought Carragher, impressed with the sound of his own voice, and with the speed of his chattering probably off his head on speed or coke.

'Now, that was very kind of you to deliver, what, guns and stuff to us. And a fucking general purpose machine gun I see peaking out of that case too. Billy, want to grab some of that shit and sort what we can use, and leave the rest for the Antrim KKK to get.'

The one with the baseball bat half ran towards him. For a second he thought about grabbing him but he reckoned the speed talking leader would not care about opening up on them both. Well, time to lay on the bullshit.

With his best received pronunciation and projection of the drill ground he began to lay it on thick.

'Mr Kannibal Killing Krew, and colleagues. You may wish to be careful. The safety is off on most of those weapons, the grenades are primed and the rover's contents are booby trapped. If you want to lift anything it might take away your hands, face or legs. Wouldn't want any harm to come to you. Now, I presume you sir are leading this wee jaunt. Not sure what you were hoping to achieve, but it all seems a bit futile.

'"Now do you have a name to which I can address you by?'

The speed talker had been silent during Carragher's brief speech, perhaps a distant memory of a teacher chastising him, or naturally reticent around vocal authority.

'Errr, Tom Moore, second in command East Antrim KKK, sir.'

Carragher almost laughed at the vigilante calling him sir, but he had to maintain the bullshit and bluffing.

'Well Mr Moore, I wouldn't want Billy there to get blown up because I'm a little close to that for comfort. Private, slowly move from that car, and make sure Billy here doesn't blow us all up.'

Patterson looked confused. He knew right well the Rover

had not been booby trapped. Carragher hoped the private would keep his mouth shut and move. It was a gamble he had not fully assessed yet, but there may be brief second if Patterson walked between Moore and him.

'Now, private, quick, I don't think Mr Moore is the patient type.'

As Patterson began to walk he noted the vigilante hands had relaxed on the AK 47. The ones with pistols seemed more at ease, thinking they were in control and still trying to figure out what Carragher had been talking about.

As soon as Billy crossed in front of him, Carragher drew his pistol. Years upon years on the range and in shooting exercises at Hereford kicked in. Two shots to the front of the face, shift aim, two more to each of the armed men. Billy crawled in front of him, the noise of the six rounds so close to him, combined with fear had him crying. Carragher thought briefly about putting two shots into his head but instead paused.

Patterson stood with his mouth swinging open and closed. 'Patterson, load what you can into that BMW, be sharp about it.'

He grabbed the crawling man by the scruff of the collar and hauled him to his feet. He was sobbing, dirty tears running down cheeks that were glowing red as adrenaline coursed through him. It was clear that had been able to it would be flight rather than fight. Hair drenched with sweat and eyes wide, but their pupils were pinpoints. Carragher briefly wondered why they had not given Billy a firearm, but realised he didn't care. He could at least use him.

'Right, you piece of shit, you lot might think you are some sort of army, but you are nothing,' he said. 'I want you to fuck away off and tell your friends that if they get in our way, I'm going to kill them all. Every single one of them and their silly little KKK friends.'

He watched as the man began stumbling away, looking over his shoulder, as if expecting to be shot.

'I've never seen shooting like that sir,' Patterson said from somewhere behind him. He turned to see the man hauling a weapons case just as a previously unseen undead grabbed him. Before he could shoulder his rifle, the zombie sunk teeth into the private's neck. Blood flowed from the bite as fingers with the skin peeling off plunged into his arm. It was clear from the blood the zombie had bit through the ceratoid artery.

Two shots to the zombies head and it fell away, no longer able to control its arm or jaw. Patterson tried to push his hands to the spurting life force from him. His mouth tried to form words but all that came out were bubbles of blood. He fell to his knees then on to his face. The pumping blood slowed. The private was dead. Carragher was not sure if he would revive or not, but to just to be on the safe side he fired two rounds into the private's head.

Looking around he could see no more undead and began to load what weapons he could fit into the BMW.

Chapter 23

Brady believed it was pretty much a suicide mission to take on the frigate, and he could see from Allen's face that the sergeant was obeying orders with reluctance. Now they were finally on the boat he felt incredibly vulnerable. It was large enough to accommodate the 20 soldiers, with equipment with everything else already stripped out. Still against a warship it seemed puny.

The fuck up of two days ago lingered in the back of his thoughts. He wanted to scream at someone, hand them their asses, punch them in the face, but he knew that it was not anyone's fault. They were facing an enemy that did not understand when they were defeated, an enemy that was unpredictable, just like the mad mullahs of Afghanistan, but an enemy that numbered most of the population; an enemy that lacked the most of their humanity and only had hunger in its place. And there were no chance of calling up an aerial strike or concentrated artillery support.

It started so simply, a tour to where the civilians were cordoned off with the inspector to assess which soldiers and police were wiling, to undertake the assault towards Ballycastle whether by land or sea.

The land rovers where about to turn off the coast road when the hair on the back of Brady's head tingled, even before he heard the shots. He shouted at the driver to speed up and pulled his helmet on, hand instinctively reaching for his rifle. He may have been promoted, he may have sat for months behind a desk, but he was still a soldier.

When the rovers got closer to the leisure centre a wave of people was running down the road, panic in the faces of all. He ordered the driver to keep going. To his right, 100 yards away was a police officer and a soldier trying to organise the rout and failing.

The driver had slowed down in the face of the panicked masses, and he ordered him to stop but keep the engine running. The soldiers with him did not need orders, they dismounted the rover, weapons ready. He glanced back towards Bryson, and she was ordering police into what was as close to a skirmish line as it could be with civilians. Brady pushed through the running mass towards the duo who were failing to slow the surge of people.

'What's happening?' he said to them. 'Zombies sir, they pushed through the barbed wire. There's more than 100 of them, we tried holding them off, but there were too many. Corporal ordered me and her to organise moving the civilians but there were too panicked. There are about 15 up there trying to hold the zombies up, but…'

His words trailed off. Brady took a beat and began to give orders.

'Okay, you two stay here and get ready to cover us. Inspector, take one of the rovers to the castle, establish a perimeter at the castle, make sure we there are not more about. Direct the civilians towards Sea Park and get ready to fucking go yourself.'

Scanning the scene Brady decided he needed to get some sort of overview of what was happening. Scrambling on top of the rover's bonnet. It was a mess. Civilians were running pel mell, some heading to the coast, some in any direction away from the advancing zombies. A number of soldiers and police were trying to fire at the zombies, but they were only hitting a few, and the chances of getting a headshot was remote. They were absorbing the rounds, some stumbling backwards a few steps, others keeping coming.

At the edge of his vision, he saw one man who seemed more composed. He was walking, slightly crouched only raising his rifle to pick off a zombie at close range, then directing panicking civilians to the road. The way he scanned and shot demonstrated that he was not a grunt, there was some specialised training, he briefly thought that this might be the Royal Marine O'Neill had mentioned, but such thoughts would have to wait. He needed to establish some kind order to this chaos.

He keyed his radio and called to the soldiers: Retreat to the Land Rover, do it as a retreat under fire, you all know the drill."

Brady's own earpiece crackled. Amidst the gun fire and screams he struggled to hear, but from the tone it was bound to be major Carragher. From what he could make out that Carragher was asking did he need reinforcements.

'If you aren't too far return to Sea Park organise barricades, funnel civilians through the barricades. Be ready for us to becoming back at full speed.'

He prayed Bryson would be ready at the shore road if his plan was to work. He barked for soldiers and police to now run to the railway bridge, ordering his driver to reverse to that bridge. He and a corporal were at the rear of the rover, all the time thinking that an APC would have been better.

As they reached the bridge Brady ordered the rover to halt and motioned for another to wait beyond. Timing, as always was going to be key, and the moral consideration of how many people he would have to sacrifice to save the greater total. There was no way to save everyone.

He watched as a 100-metres away a zombie grabbed a soldier from the back and bit into the man's face, pulling the soldier's flesh off his nose and biting again. Seargeant Allen was near, and Brady admired the man's composure as he put two rounds into the zombie's head, looked at the slouched, injured man and put two rounds into his face. A justified mercy killing.

Chapter 24

Carragher was reflecting on that chaos two weeks on. How entire command and control system had been smashed into smithereens, and even experienced soldiers had fallen to bits. He didn't blame Brady entirely. His plan to blow up a rover under the bridge with grenades and petrol cannisters was sound enough in theory but was not enough to stem the flow of the undead.

He sighed, thinking for the first time since he was ordered back to base, what seemed an eternity earlier, and briefed by a colonel whose face was grey that the talk of zombies was real, that they were to seal off the barracks and prepare for further orders. The colonel finished saying God go with them before drawing his pistol and shooting himself through the mouth.

For a man who had seen so much in special forces and done much more he was shocked in the calm and collected colonel manner he had shot himself. It affected Carragher more than much else since that day. He suspected he had been in survival mode since. In three or four African or Arabian cess pools he had been active in, the major had been in that same mode; concentrating on the task, adrenaline almost constantly flowing, a few special 'pills' to keep the edge, before the inevitable collapse once the mission was complete.

Now he sat astride a motorbike scanning the coast as Brady's packed boat bumbled its way out of a marina of stranded boats. Carragher could momentarily reflect on the different leadership styles of the general and Greg. Both took advice, but only one really listened. One weighed up each decision. He suspected the trio of Sam, Smicker and Seamus served as a sounding board. Even when he arrived and had tried to assert some sort of relevant control Greg had been open to his suggestions and yet he believed the trio had been who he listened to more, as he weighed up what action to take.

And he never gave orders, just possible courses of action to take. It seemed to him that Sam was the one turning those actions into orders, which for a twenty something woman was remarkable in and of itself. He couldn't get a bead on Smicker and his wise cracking. Seamus was another matter. The man was clearly the Royal Marine O'Neill and subsequently Brady described. Part of 43 Commando? Or one of the other elements of the marines that were assigned to work with the SBS and others as the punch and power of the special force units when needed.

Carragher had disobeyed in terms of the exact orders during the chaos in Carrick. Once he had roused the soldiers and police at Sea Park into action and issued orders he had overseen the ramshackle barricade, he took a rover towards Carrick and was only marginally surprised when he saw Knifer stood on the back of a small truck, Lee Enfleld strapped on his shoulder, pistol drawn and held downwards at ready. The man was a ghost, but a valuable one. His only motivation seemed to be survival and safety for the few that he appeared to care for.

As he tried to assess again everything that happened, he took the small notepad from his shoulder pocket. He had always had a notepad with him, scribbling in it to clarify his thoughts, tearing up each page, or burning it entirely as soon as a couple of pages were filled. He did not need to make notes on the two men at the top of each group, but he needed to make a few notes to decide his course of action. He had briefed Brady on the fact that those heading to Ballycastle to meet the Icelandic boats and assured him he would keep overwatch from the high ground. He did not say who he would be keeping overwatch for.

He also noted down just the name Knifer. An unknown quantity, a warrior but one from one of the more secretive branches of the military, those rumoured to be more elite than the rest of the elite forces. As he jotted down the name his mind flicked to the image of the pickup truck ploughing through people, alive and undead alike, Knifer urging the driver to keep going, as he fired rounds into the heads of zombies, despite being on the back of a moving vehicle. He himself was busy gesturing to soldiers to escort the civilians to Sea Park to see when Knifer's vehicle disappeared from view behind the retreating Land Rovers of Brady and Bryson. It was Bryson who took the decisive action to restore order to the chaotic retreat.

Her vehicle had slowed to a crawl and she jumped off. A quick glance around and she raised her Heckler and Koch and loosed off two bursts into the air. The crowd stopped and ducked in an automatic response. "Walk quickly, do not run. Walk with a soldier or police officer nearby. Walk towards me."

The inspector's authority in her barked orders had the desired effect, not calming the crowd down entirely, but at least stopping the rout.

Carragher pushed the top cover of his rover open and began to scan for targets. It was clear that many of the civilians would not make it through the barricades before they were overrun by what seemed like an increasing horde of the undead.

A phalanx of soldiers and several police officers were shielding Brady and Bryson, the soldiers seemed to be from the 16 Airbourne as they were demonstrating discipline in picking out targets and nudging the civilians out of the line of fire.

Brady was through the barricade first, barking out for Sergeant Allen. When he spotted the sergeant he spoke briefly, Carragher didn't hear what was said, too busy trying to estimate how many they could save before they had to abandon their position. He watched as two police officers uncoiled razor wire. Shouting to them to close the gap to their right he heard several shots from the direction of Sea Park.

What the fuck now he thought.

It was two minutes later he saw Allen pushing a zombie at the end of a long stick, presumably the sasumata he had described, with another soldier pushed a pole to direct the stumbling horror towards where he had directed the police officers to close the gap. His mind tumbled wondering and puzzled until he saw another zombie being urged along and Brady gesturing. He had to know…

He jumped down from his vantage point: "What the fuck sir?"

"The ones the late Colonel O'Neill had detained might be attracting the others. These two we are going to push into the midst of the too slow, or two stupid to follow Bryson's lead."

"Are you seriously talking about sacrificing civilians?"

"And anyone else who can't make it through the line Bryson is holding. We have neither the time nor resources to accommodate them all, and we have orders."

Carragher swore under his breath as he saw the two zombies pushed through the wire, and further still until they swung their decaying frames towards those too uncoordinated to find or see the exit from the melee.

'Major, I believe you have a mission to fulfil?'

He barked out a yes sir and gathered the private and sergeant to set out for Ballymena.

MDK 187

'Murder, Death Kill
Welcome to the purge'

Cursed Sun

Part Three

Racing

Chapter 1

Sam was trying to keep her thoughts from roaming through the possible horror of failing. She recalled the games of chess she had with Greg as they waited for departure. Remembering his 'tell' when he sensed an opportunity, a brief scratch of the nose, followed by a hand through his hair. The pause to sip a drink. Usually, it was two or three moves later he saw the trap she had laid. For such a strategist she had beaten him every time until he refused to play her again and huffed until he had beaten Smicker or Seamus.

Was this mad dash to Ballycastle comparable? Was her mini-convoy or Jen's the sacrificial piece? Or were Greg and the rest who were staying sacrificing themselves as a diversion? Would any opponents they face fall or checkmate their plans.

Such thoughts weren't helpful she knew, as they waited while the tractor, two vehicles ahead, pushed a car from their path with the adapted snow plough. She glanced around to see Tom walking among their passengers, offering small talk.

Her load was a mixture of children, teens and adults. Trauma had, in brief, been suspended by being on the move, however she had begun to see the signs among the smaller ones. There were growing quieter. Ruth and Tom were with them, trying to keep them engaged, but even the chit chat among the teens was ebbing too. Only JoJo seemed to be alert, clutching his rifle with the one round. Yes, his face showed fear, but he was keeping his eyes on the windows. She saw them flick forwards and she turned to see Jude hopping from his tractor, waving them to stop..

'There's a mess of cars up ahead, we're going to drive through with the snow blade, then we'll need to take a break to refuel," he explained. "Take it slow behind us, 50 metre gap.'

Sam nodded in understanding and Elijah, behind the wheel acknowledged.

'He can be a bit anal, can't he?'

He was right, Jude could be a bit uptight and precise. That combined with his lanky frame and babyish face all but screamed, geek. They watched the tractor begin to push through two smashed cars and Sam all but swore when she saw a zombie in one, dead decaying fingers scrawling at the window, trapped in eternal hunger.

When they got past the five wrecks Jude had already stopped and was busy with the jerry cans. Rambo had dismounted and was moving his rifle back and forwards as if he knew what he was doing.

She and Tom dismounted, and she noted that Tom had merely unclipped the strap on his side arm and kept his own rifle shouldered. But his eyes were flicking back and forth.

They were just past Carnlough and Tom gestured over his shoulder with a movement of his hand. She turned slowly, and noticed what he had seen, a boat about half a mile from shore. With a casual gesture he handed Sam binoculars.

She walked slowly to the rear of the bus, crouched and watched, before raising the binoculars. It was a boat packed with soldiers. An older man in uniform was gesturing behind where they had stopped and on the radio to someone. She didn't like those gestures and was thankful that they were mostly concealed by hedges.

'Tom, I don't like this one little bit, we need to get moving, pronto,' she said. 'I think there are people behind us, who knows what, but I don't want to find out.

'Jude, just finish it now, we need to move now.'

Pulling the jerry can away from the tractor's fuel tank he raised his eyebrows and was about to ask a question.

'I think we're being followed, and there is a boat full of soldiers over there. I don't want to find out what they want.'

Throwing the cannister to the side of the road she watched

as two zombies came from the weed-choked undergrowth and seized at Rambo. He screamed as one tried to bite his shoulder and fired his rifle, spinning from the impetus of the second zombie. His weapon was on full automatic. Rounds ricocheted off the cliffs and then hit the tractor and the bus. Tom waited until the clip was empty then moved forward. He shot the zombies in the head, grimacing as grey matter splattered over his trousers.

Sam joined hm staring at Rambo. He was groaning, eyes pleading at her, mouth moving slowly, as blood spilled over his lips.

'Well, Corporal Jones, I knew you wouldn't make it to Ballycastle, but this wasn't what I was thinking of.' She shot him in the head twice. Tom merely glanced at her, then she heard the screaming from behind them.

As she ran time slowed to a crawl. A part of her knew it was the mind trying to absorb information, adrenaline fuelled fight or flight as she ran to the bus door. The screaming went on, the piercing shrill of children's cries mixed with angered howls. She froze at the door, took a deep breath, closed her eyes for a second, then stepped forward.

Elijah was blocking her vision, but from the way he was standing, shoulders slumped she knew this was not going to be good. Pushing him aside Sam gasped. Ruth was lying over two of the children, blood oozing from her stomach, blood coming from each side of her mouth. Nudging Elijah, she lifted her gently off the children. One had a wound to his arm. The other was clearly dead, half his skull lying on his shoulder.

'She jumped on top of them to save them," JoJo said. "As soon as the shots started she shouted get down and jumped across them all. Fuck! Fuck! Fuck!'

'JoJo, take a breath, deep, good. Now go to the door. Tell Tom and explain to him we need to take care of them, and then we move. Understand?'

He nodded and moved, stopping for a second to look at the bodies. A single tear welling in his left eye, as he walked to the front of the bus. Sam bent to Ruth, this fragile girl, dealing with demons, surviving so long in this hell.

She bent and Ruth grasped her arm, pulled her close to her mouth. Involuntary revulsion to being so close, eased, and Ruth tried to smile. The phrase rictus grin popped into Sam's mind.

'I did good Sam,' Ruth said in a whisper. 'I did.'

'Yes, you did,' Sam said, as she watched the light go from Ruth's eyes.

She knelt beside the teenager's body for a moment, feeling that she was about to be overwhelmed, but knowing she couldn't yet. The rest of the bus, the others, the boat offshore of them, whatever was behind them, and the certainty she would try to keep them going forward to Ballycastle.

'Elijah, help me. JoJo go to the back of the bus. You see anything you shout. Tell Tom to get on the radio to Greg and tell Jude to get ready to move.'

He nodded and moved, glad to be doing something, as she grabbed under Ruth's shoulders, Elijah lifted her legs, and they shuffled their way off. Tom saw them, and uttered one word, "Jesus". The anger she had been keeping from herself burst.

"Jesus wasn't here, Jesus didn't help Ruth, Jesus didn't fucking save anyone. Now Tom you have a job to do, fucking do it."

The big former policeman gazed back at her and said "Yes M'am"

That this experienced cop, 40 years older, should call her M'am broke her fury. Her mind was still operating in what seemed like a crawl at the horror, but she knew that it would spill over sooner or later.

As she and Elijah went towards the back of the bus she nodded for JoJo to return onboard. Laying Ruth's body at the edge of the road, she asked the man she regarded as a friend could he bring the other dead child. As he moved off she sobbed, she couldn't remember the name of the dead boy, just his smashed face.

Tom was walking towards her, radio to his ear as Eijah was laying the boy' body beside Ruth.

'Someone wants to talk to you,' he said. 'Okay, but you have to move the everyone forward around that bend, now.

She held the radio, watching the mini-convoy move. As soon as they were out of sight she clicked the button on the radio: 'One second.' And clicked it off as the voice started to reply. Looking down at Ruth's body she took in a shivering breath before firing into the teenager's head.

'I don't know if it will help but you won't become one of them.'

She clicked the radio as she drew in breath to stop her own scream.

'What?'

'Ach, we got the usual shit, zombies, paramilitaries, soldiers, all good fun. What's up with you?'

Smicker, as always making light, but now she hadn't time.

'We've three dead, soldiers on a boat near us and somebody coming up behind us on the road. Any chance of some support?'

'Where are you?'

As she filled him in, she could hear him grow serious.

'Listen Jenny got into a total shitstorm too, no casualties but we had to ride into the rescue. Greg can maybe get to you in about half an hour, but he'll be pushing it.'

'Okay, send him. who's with him.'

With that detail sorted she just signed off with a see you in Ballycastle and jogged to the bus. Tom was waiting by the door.

'That took real guts Sam. Promise me you'll do the same if I'm hit?'

Nodding she went to the door. He put his arm around her and whispered, 'The kids are really messed up."

'So am I,' she said. "They'll need sugar and drinks once the shock kicks in. Watch for any shivering. We'll need to move now.'

Elijah sounded the horn and Jude began to move the tractor. She looked around the children. Several were looking at her, but most had vacant looks as they stared into space. She knew it would take a moment for her to slip into same fugue, but she had to concentrate.

Boobytrap the road, put barriers up, stop to find out who it was. Thoughts tumbled, and she couldn't seem to stop them, careening, until she felt a tap on her shoulder. It was JoJo.

'Will we make it,' he said as he pushed up his glasses.

'Yes, we will, we must.' She realised once again the responsibility that she had, the leadership she had accepted and now would gladly relinquish. She reached out to hold the young man's shoulder and noticed the tremble in her hand before human contact seemed to ease it.

'Listen JoJo, I need everyone like you alert. Did you see anything?'

Shaking his head he stammered that he thought he heard engines. She drew him into a hug they both needed. Breaking off, she asked him to keep again to keep watch. As the bus moved off she picked up Tom's binoculars again and tried to monitor what was out to sea. As they came round a headland, she spotted it again and found she was staring at someone watching her on their own set of binoculars. He was probably in his late 50s, in full battle fatigue, slightly overweight, but his bearing shouted command. He took down his binoculars and seemed to issue orders, gesturing to somewhere behind them. Whatever he had ordered she believed she noticed the bow edge the craft closer to the shore.

CHAPTER 2

Carragher had been doing what he promised, keeping overwatch. Given the elevation had plenty of areas he could see the boat, the refugee's vehicles and the three land rovers behind them; one in khaki army, two in police white. Gauging the relative speeds, they would catch up within 30 minutes, and maybe sooner as the tractor with the snowplough was clearing a path through abandoned vehicles that was impossible to close.

As ordered, he had been keeping radio silence but listened in to the relatively few communications between Brady and Bryson. Then when Brady spotted the bus and tractor the tone of the already terse communications changed. The general ordered Bryson to catch up and detain the vehicle's occupants and 'authorised' the use of lethal force if necessary. If they agreed to be detained, they were to be turned around and sent to Carrick. In other words, another death sentence given what little living had been left in the town.

Half expecting Bryson to agree, while hoping she would decline, he listened to her reply.

'We are not a death squad general," she said. "I agreed to prevent or delay them from reaching Ballycastle. I will do that. If we are fired upon, we will respond, but no-one will be executed while I command this leg of the operation. And I for one will not be returning to Carrick to deal with that infestation.'

Bryson words made Carracher realise then that for all his equivocation he would not be providing overwatch for the general but would be for the escapees from Ballymena. Would that be committing treason? Technically yes but here at what passed for the end of the world there would not be any court martials. Kangaroo courts were more likely to be the norm, with summarily deadly judgments carried out facing the barrels of guns.

Pushing his motorbike forward 400 metres ahead of the closing convoys. He dismounted and snuggled into a crevice before siting his sniper rifle. Satisfied, he peered at the boat though his binoculars. Bryson seemed to have gathered together a mixture of police, local soldiers and 12 Air Assault. Carragher recognised a few, some he had served with and in what was normal warfare were capable warriors, but only in terms of obeying orders. And one was a vicious bastard who had almost been kicked out several times for his sheer brutality to friend or foe. That man would have no problem joining a firing squad, or just stabbing the person Brady showed a dislike for.

Then he noticed Sergeant Allen in the boat. The rugged Northern Irish man had displayed both intelligence, insight and decisiveness. Now his frame was slightly slumped, he was not watching the shoreline but gazing out to sea. The major guessed, with some certainty, that he was doubting the wisdom of the general's plan, and his casual attitude in issuing orders relating to lethal force.

CHAPTER 3

As they turned the corner to take the road to Ballycastle there was a pick-up truck across the road, steam pouring out of the engine. A man was hunkered near the engine. On the bed of the truck stood a weird mixture of soldier and hippie. Straggly, brown hair tumbled over his shoulders, stubble flecked face, wearing a combat jacket and torn jeans. He had a rifle over his shoulder.

As the tractor pulled close, he raised the rifle.

Sam ordered them all to stop. Getting off the bus she pulled the pistol but didn't raise it. She gestured to those that had also dismounted to keep weapons lowered. The last thing they needed was an accidental shoot-out.

'Can we help you,' she said. The man hopped with ease from the vehicle.

'Depends,' he said. 'You space for four more in your little convoy?'

'Depends,' she replied. 'Depends on who you are and what you want.'

'Well, my name is Knifer, those are Suzanne, Billy and Big Joe. As to what we want. To get the fuck as far to the north coast as possible and get the fuck away from that mad general, zombies and the fucking vigilantes. I've watched two close friends being eaten and one shot by some former vigilantes, Former, as we killed them. Self-defence sort of thing.'

He had lowered the rifle as he spoke and then shouldered it.

Sam holstered her own weapon and gestured for those behind her to do the same. She called Tom forward.

'Tom, this Mr Knifer, and that is Suzanne, Billy and Big Joe. They want a lift.'

The big police man was about to respond when the

soldier/hippie said: 'It's just Knifer, not a mister. We can only offer some beer and four people that know how to handle weapons. We have seen enough shit, and the last thing I want is to get into a row.

'There's a squad of soldiers and police behind you, and to be honest the last thing I think any of us needs is an argument with guns.'

Tom asked how many beers. But before Knifer could answer Sam interrupted.

'Okay, we are going as far as Ballycastle, we can drop you off when we get close, or you can join us where we are going. And no beers until we get there. Deal?'

'Deal, we can squeeze in somewhere, I'm sure.'

Sam wasn't sure who or what they were, but this man had a bearing that spoke of steel in his core.

As the other three came forward, shaking hands she said to Tom: 'Beer? Are you turning into Smicker?'

Once on their way Knifer explained the chaos in Carrick, the general turning zombies onto civilians, and the plan to stop "some navy ship going astray."

Sam wasn't sure how much to tell him of the Icelandic offer just yet, but she suspected that the Iceland boats would welcome the man she sat beside. He didn't say who or what he was, but she suspected he had seen service, much like Seamus, in an elite branch of the army or navy.

CHAPTER 4

Brady was raging. His authority was being challenged by a civilian, police officer or not. He had been given the authority by the current head of government. Whether anyone liked it or not, the country was being governed by the army, and he was the army's choice to govern Northern Ireland. Therefore, in his mind, the police came under his command. He was pissed off enough by being sent on this futile mission to stop the charge of the civilians to Ballycastle and seize back the frigate.

Added into the mix was some of the men on the mission, Sergeant Allen being one he had most concern over. Before boarding the boat, Allen had been worked well with him, and apart from a few issues, he had obeyed orders and been a useful sounding board, as well as a capable senior NCO. Moving closer to their target he had been noticeably distant, often just staring out to sea or looking down at his boots. Yes, he followed the infrequent orders since leaving Carrick, but the spark he had noticed when they first met was gone. He had even hesitated for a couple of seconds connecting Brady to Bryson.

The man at the helm, Duffy he recalled, had been smoking away, his only demand to take them there was a case of beer and multiple packets of cigarettes. He hadn't touched the beer but had been chugging from a hip flask. Brady did not know who or what he was before, but all he cared about was that he did what he was told.

Fuck it, he thought, you can only do what you can do.

'Right sergeant, pull yourself together and gather the other NCOs,' he said. 'We need to go over our best plan of attack.'

'Yes, sir' was the lacklustre response.

Before moving, Allen said: 'Sir, may I say something, with

regards to where we are and what happens next.'

Brady nodded for Allen to continue.

'Sir, even with the best luck in the world and we hit the frigate with the LAW-80, we would have to board it while whatever crew was doing damage control. It would only take a few sailors or same mad Icelandic bastard to hold us off. None of us has the experience of hostile boarding, we're not marines.

'As I see it we can move to intercept the civilians. With Bryson behind we can land close to Ballycastle and stop them in their tracks. Without the civilians the frigate has no mission, it can sail off to Iceland and the navy can go take it back when it suits them, and this shit is over."

Brady found his hand drifting to his holster, thinking that no NCO had spoken to him so directly since he was a young junior lieutenant. But he also knew he had asked Allen to speak freely, and what was relevant was the fact that the bones of what the sergeant said was true.

However, what the sergeant did not know was he had no intention of boarding the frigate. What the sergeant did not know was deep in the hold of this boat was 20 kilos of explosive. All he needed to do was distract the crew with missile, tie a rope to the lock the rudder and prop, abandon the boat, swim for shore and await the boom. It wouldn't sink the frigate, or injure many aboard, but would put it out of action.

'Sergeant, I think we all know that it is a desperate mission. I am under direct command of the CIC, and he, for now, is in charge of what is left of this country.

'I have a plan, but for now I assure you that when the time comes you and everybody else will abandon ship as soon as I say. Float ashore and hope we are still can still fight when we need to.'

'Yes sir, I understand.'

What he understood he did not say, just went to gather the other NCOs.

What Brady understood was that some soldiers might not make it off this boat. He wished he hadn't been given been given this poisoned command chalice. He also wished he had Major Caragher on the boat, but he was content he was at least on overwatch. When the time came he would order him to spread chaos on those he wanted to subdue.

CHAPTER 5

Carragher judged that it would take just 20 minutes for the joint police and army unit to catch up to what Carragher now simply dubbed the survivors. He boarded his motorcycle and went along the rugged clifftop. Guessing that the survivors would not risk their mini convoy along the Fair Head's Dyke, as it would be too steep, and instead would take the main road and be out of sight from the boat. No doubt Bryson would make the same guess.

As he moved cautiously along the treacherous path, he wondered what a Royal Marine, from one of their specialist units had been doing in Northern Ireland, and why this rag tag bunch of survivors had managed to acquire so much firepower, and specialist weapons like the sniper rifles.

Sure, he had provided some as part of his cover, but he could imagine some good kit from their varied raids on army barracks and police stations, but there was an unprecedented concentration. Now there was this Knifer. He looked like a combination of a CIA deep cover trainer, and a veteran of the SAS, but his bearing suggested much else. There had always been rumours among all special forces across the world that above them was another unit of 'ghosts'. Trained to an even higher level and with missions that were plausibly deniable by government and armed forces.

As Carragher pulled up the motorbike, he tried to think of this Knifer with short hair and holding himself to attention, or marching. Something was nagging him, somewhere at the back of his mind.

His contemplation ended as his radio pinged; Brady speaking before the major had it to his ear.

'Carragher, where are you?'

'Overwatch on the joint army and police unit pursuing the defenders.'

'Good, now I do not know what Bryson has planned, but you need to make sure that the civilian convoy does not reach Ballycastle. I cannot tell you the exact details, but the north coast of this forsaken fucking island will be of strategic importance once we get over this current crisis.

'I don't care what you have to do, or who you have to shoot, just get it done. Understand?'

'Very much so, sir, I understand you,' Carragher replied now confident that he would delight in putting a round through Brady's face. This was not a war zone, he had been given an order to shoot on what were essentially British and Irish civilians who were combatants by accident, who as far as he knew only used their weapons in self-defence. Their only mission seemed to be survival. Brady was in 'obeying orders' mode, and it would be his excuse if he was ever held to account for the multiple deaths.

Nestling down to a position where he could observe an open space of road he began the adjustments to his sight, the calculations in his head to allow for wind and temperature. They were probably superfluous measurements at this range, being less than 500 yards from the road, but they helped calm him.

At the distant sound of engines, he swung round to see that the survivors' convoy had stopped and were busy arranging the vehicles in a defensive position. Greg had joined them from fuck knows where, Sam was ushering children to small ditches beside the road, and Knifer was helping adults get into safer firing points

Chapter 6

As the sound of their pursuers came closer Sam took a decision that they were not going to be able to outrun them before they reached Ballycastle. She arranged what she hoped would be enough for protection. The tractor with the snowplough facing the direction their pursuers were coming from, the buses arranged behind it. All the children were in the minibus in the rear, under the watchful eyes of Tom and JoJo.

Greg arrived just before they stopped and Sam had at first deferred to him, but he said it was her show. He walked along their lines he introduced himself to Knifer.

'I'm Greg, sort of the one-time leader of this group'" he said. 'Have you decided to join us in this shitshow trying to get to Ballycastle? Or is this just an opportunist way to boost your chances?'

Knifer stared straight into the former teacher's eyes. Greg had taught one or two teens who had stared at him like that. One became a paramilitary and died a violent death. The other had been a certified psycho in Greg's mind but had gone on to run of the biggest investment funds in the world. A momentary shudder went down Greg's spine, but he kept locked with Knifer's eyes.

'Haven't decided yet,' he said. 'And I suspect that Ballycastle isn't your final destination. I think there's more to this wee jaunt than running away. What I know there is more empathy here than that mad bastard general who thinks he is running the country and is quite happy to see children and adults die equally. So, for the time being I'm throwing my lot in with you, at least until you tell me what the fuck you are doing.'

Greg reached forward and shook the man's hand. It was a

straightforward gesture and Knifer looked momentarily ill-at-ease as if he had never had his hand shaken before.

They were turning to face the lines when Sam ushered them back behind the defensive line. One tractor, flanked by two upturned cars, the buses to the rear. Eljah and Jude had the machine guns trained down the road. Knifer had taken up position with his colleagues beside one of the cars; elsewhere there were rifles poking out of hedges and debris.

As she looked at the position she stepped forward into the middle of the road. Greg yelled for her to get back, but she just shrugged and moved forward, 10 metres in front of the tractor's snowplough.

She braced herself as the first of the Land Rovers rounded the corner, keeping her rifle on her shoulder. Sam recalled Seamus telling her he wasn't a great shot, but she reckoned if she wasn't killed instantly she could use her fire as a distraction for the others to open fire. Fuck this is foolish, she thought, but if I'm to help lead then I have to show them all that I will risk myself.

All three Land Rovers were now lined up like an arrow pointed toward her.

Sam took a deep breath and did the only things she could think of: she smiled and waved a greeting as a police officer in full tactical gear and a soldier dismounted from the lead vehicle.

Behind them what seemed a well-disciplined group formed themselves to cover the ground.

Chapter 7

Carragher didn't like the defensive position they had managed to put together. Knifer had organised turning the wrecked cars sideways on, but he surely knew that rifle bullets would carve through aluminium straight into the flesh of anyone sheltering behind. He trained his sights on the soldier flanking Bryson. He had his weapon trained on Sam, but not yet looking to aim. He decided that if there was a firefight he would be the first to go down, but he wasn't about to do anything that would precipitate an ill-matched battle.

Close enough he heard Sam call out, as he marvelled at her courage.

'"Hi there, hope you don't mind but we sort of need to know what you are and what you want,' she said. 'You see we were here going about our lawful wee drive to the seaside, and you lot appear. Jesus, we've had enough trouble with zombies, and truth be told we are a bit suspicious of the police and army right now.'

Bryson looked as if she was struggling to keep from smiling, but then her face hardened.

'I am under orders from the current head of Northern Ireland's government to detain you and stop you from moving beyond this spot,' the inspector said. 'Alternatively, you can remain here of your own freewill and we will proceed to our destination.'

Sam then laughed. 'Ach we could let you pass through but there's a wee problem. My colleagues here have imposed a toll to use this road, as per nobody gives a fuck about who's in government. Call it private enterprise, but it is two beers for every adult and a packet of crisps and a coke for the kids.'

The soldier beside Bryson said: 'Are you fucking kidding?'

'No,' said Sam. 'Of course not, but you all seem a little

tense, thought you might need a laugh.'

'I think we all are,' replied Bryson. 'I'm not sure I got your name. I'm Inspector Bryson and although I've no papers to prove it I was given orders by the de facto head of government. Are you in charge of this group?'

Sam thought for a second, there was the need for a bluff, or some smart answer.

'My name is Sam, and I suppose I am leader of this group, though not by choice, more due to my fantastic organisational skills."

CHAPTER 8

Carragher had been listening in through the open line Bryson had kept on. No doubt Brady was too. He rested his rifle and went to lift his binoculars. As he did, he caught distant movement to his right, on the road Bryson had come along. Standing up he trained his binoculars on the winding road, two miles back.

'Fuck,' he muttered to himself. There was a ragtag collection of vehicles, all with KKK emblazoned on them. The lead red pick-up truck had a heavy machine gun mounted over the cab in a configuration much like many he had seen in then the middle east, and Africa. He scanned behind Sam's position to check if there were more KKK. 'Ach for fuck sake.' There was about 30 or so zombies stumbling down the road from the opposite direction.

'Inspector Bryson. This is Carragher. I want you to listen very closely and if you can relay what I say to Sam too. It is of immediate concern. Behind you approaching your position is a convoy of those vigilante pricks, the KKK. Behind Sam's position is a group of zombies.

'The vigilantes are of more immediate concern. They are in six vehicles the lead vehicle has a heavy machine gun mounted on the cab. They will be within sight in five minutes. Get the NCOs with you to arrange the Land Rovers in a defensive posture.

'Tell Sam to move her vehicles 50 yards away from you.'

He paused, to still the slight catch in his throat. 'I will take out the man on the machine gun as soon as they come within visual range, then your officers and the soldiers open up with everything.

'Sam needs to turn her vehicles to face where the zombies are coming. Once they have sight of them tell them to use their machine gun and mow down every one of them, we'll deal with headshots later.'

Without hesitation Bryson replied 'Understood'.

He knew from his time in the special forces that all ranks needed a clear tasking from officers, and NCOs relied on that tasking to achieve the mission. He had pissed off so many officers by insisting on going on missions to learn from the NCOs and what they needed.

'Carragher,' Brady interrupted his thoughts and sighting his weapon. 'You are jeopardising the mission. Those civilians are to be stopped not helped.'

'Sir, please go fuck yourself. Maybe you've forgotten about situational awareness, but this is a situation with lives of soldiers, police and civilians are at stake. Now, go sail your boat and do whatever you think you can do.'

'I'll have your head for that Carragher. You are going to be one dead cunt very soon.'

With that, he clicked off and the boat adjusted its course. As he adjusted his position. he saw Bryson gesture silent applause to where she thought he must be. He was 30 metres from where she was gesturing, but no matter right now.

He checked the progress of the vigilantes, sighted the point where they would come into visual contact, and began the delicate measurements and adjustments.

CHAPTER 9

Bryson relayed the information and Carragher's instructions. Sam had caught some of it, but she turned, called Greg, Tom and Knifer over.

'You trust him?' Knifer and Tom said at the same time.

'He told that general to fuck off, that's enough for me. I think he is straight up this time, and I think that we don't have any options. There are vigilantes that way and zombies that way.

She relayed the plan and before she could finish Greg was turning to get the vehicles moved.

Knifer said he would get as high as he could to give cover in both directions. She watched them move, and for a second wondered what she was doing. Was she to go to the forward firing line, was she to organise the children, was she to…she didn't know. What she could do was to oversee what they were doing, give words of encouragement, then help Tom shelter the children.

She shouted to Jude and Elijah telling them to turn their tractor and machine guns towards the road ahead 'as quick as you fucking can'.

Greg jogged back to her, put his arm on her shoulder, and just said, 'you're going to be okay'. It was the simple touch that was enough to shake off the immediate fear.

Chapter 10

The lead vehicle of the vigilantes was moving slow enough for Carragher to track as it came to the point they would spot the Land Rovers. He adjusted again for the elevation and the mild breeze. Deep inside he held a shallow breath, and as he released felt the familiar tension before taking a shot at this range. He did his best to blank out the previous times he had watched a body fall after he pulled the trigger, or the tension in the hours firing at targets on the range and seeing each victim on the cardboard shapes.

The truck reached the point. He fired. The man standing at the heavy machine gun twitched and slumped over the gun. His back was a twisted mass of red.

Soldiers and police officers opened fire. He picked another target, and another vigilante fell.

The vehicles tried to reverse, Carragher aimed at the rear most vehicle, pumping rounds into its occupants and its bodywork. They were now stuck in the fire being laid down from the Land Rovers' occupants and the now broken-down car to the rear. They had two choices: surrender or fight and die.

Chapter 11

Sam understood the term fight or flight; she also knew that the concept of time slowing down in traumatic situations. She knew her brain was flooding with chemicals, her adrenal glands were in overdrive, she knew all this, and more, but the lecture theatre and the here and now were different. There had been nothing in the previous hectic weeks to equal this chaos. The first shot froze her to the spot, the fusillade from the soldiers and police broke the spell, and she was running to the side of the bus with the children. It was too exposed to the sporadic fire coming from the vigilantes. She signalled for it to pull in closer to the rock face. Elijah, Jude and Knifer were concentrating on keeping the zombies at bay. Knifer and his colleagues were picking out headshots, the rest just spraying what seemed like a growing horde.

She heard a scream from the Land Rovers "RPG! RPG!" Her mind shouted Rocket Propelled Grenade and she felt her body crouch and tuck itself into the side of bus. And then the explosion. She saw with clarity shards of shrapnel flying past her, she felt a sting in her leg and reached down to feel a hot graze. She saw an arm land a foot in front of her, still grasping a rifle. Her ears were ringing, but she watched Knifer switch his attention and move forwards towards the remaining Land Rovers. He was picking his shots. From above Carragher laid down more fire. She glanced in the bus, the children were all crouched down, apart from JoJo, who was poking his rifle through a broken window. She gave him a thumbs up and there was a half-smile, half-grimace on his face. Then she heard a scream.

Less than five yards away Tom was being bitten by one of the undead. Its teeth were clamped on his shoulder, its hands were pushing into the policeman's face. He was fumbling to raise his pistol. Sam stood and walked to the horrible coupling. She raised her gun and shot the zombie on the side of its head. Its grey arms fell away from Tom's face, but its teeth were lodged in the flesh of Tom's shoulder. Tom looked at her. There was what, as the cliché said, a look of resignation in his eyes. He smiled to her, said "good luck" and shot himself in the side of the head. She saw his skull explode outwards, shards of bone and bloodied brain flew outwards. She let loose a cry as the man and the undead fell as one, two more corpses.

A shot behind her. JoJo had fired at two more zombies that were crawling from the undergrowth. He had missed. She shouted to him to stay in the bus, and as she shouted emotions strange to her swept through her: protectiveness towards the children; grief at Tom's death; and rage. A real red mist, her eyes stung.

She walked to the crawling undead, As they grasped at her she raised her gun and shot each through the head. She turned to where Elijah and Jude were trying to keep the horde at bay. She picked up a rifle lying by the bus and fired an entire clip towards the horde. Sam then ordered Jude to drive the tractor straight at them to plough them aside.

CHAPTER 12

Carragher was still firing at the KKK vehicles as the soldiers and police tied to re-group after the Land Rover was hit by the RPG. He was running low on ammunition, so he propelled himself down the hill, slipping, stumbling and almost falling headfirst at one point. At the foot of the hill, he paused hearing shots to his left and decided that he needed to help eliminate the enemy that had weapons first.

Bryson was trying to organise her group, but she had no military background. The three surviving police officers looked dazed, as did a number of the soldiers. He shook one and pointed to where he wanted him.

All but one of the vigilantes' vehicles were riddled by bullet holes and more than dozen bodies lay beside them. Still one vehicle's occupants were firing. Grabbing a rifle, he lined up two shots. The first hit an unwary man in centre mass. The second grazed a heavyset woman's arm.

He was looking for a target when a shout came: "Stop, stop, stop, we surrender".

Carragher indicated the soldiers still standing to ceasefire.

'Stand up, put your arms in the air, walk slowly to us,' he said. 'Try something stupid and you'll be killed.'

Three men and the wounded woman emerged, and walked, arms raised. Two still had the stupid white headband with KKK scrawled on it. They looked confused as they glanced to their fallen.

'Inspector, as ranking civilian officer present, can you detain these,' he said. 'And take those stupid headbands off. We will want to ask some questions later.'

Bryson nodded and with another officer waited until they were closer. Carragher hadn't seen where she had lifted handcuffs from but two were cuffed and the other couple had their hands bound with their own headbands. They were pushed to the ground, and Carragher turned towards the fire in the other direction.

The bus was intact, but one of the tractors was now driving into the horde, its attached snowplough pushing aside the undead and crushing others.

He was running towards the scene, watching as Greg tried to pull Sam back. She shrugged him aside. An AKM rifle in her hands she was shooting the zombies in the head, with a single shot, not seeming to worry that they were close enough to grasp. With each shot she let loose a guttural yell. He saw that she would soon be overwhelmed. Knifer was now at the other side of the tractor and he was coping well, dispatching those undead around him with calm ease.

'Greg, help her,' he said as he drew within yards of the man. Stopping he grabbed a discarded handgun. It was loaded, and he began o take aim at those undead closest to Sam. Greg had snapped out of whatever daze he had been in and began firing. There were no headshots, but it was slowing some down. He shouted up for the tractor to reverse, looked at Knifer and he nodded.

There were still 20 or so undead stumbling their way. Knifer pushed Greg's gun down, then took it, walking towards the reduced horde. They walked in step, taking shots, first at those closest to Sam, then picking them off. He shot five more before he heard the click of the empty gun. Knifer hit another eight, before drawing is own handgun and tossing it to Carragher, as he pulled a machete from a pouch on his back.

Sam was now facing three undead, and seemed to have used all her ammunition. She had frozen just pointing the rifle as they came closer. Caragher had sight of two and brought them down. Sam was blocking his aim for the third. He watched as she raised the rifle and brought the butt into the top of the zombie's head, raised it again and the second blow saw the undead now laid to rest in a pool of yellow muck.

She looked at him. Her eyes were glazed, her mouth shaped in an 'O' as she sucked in air. She glanced to her side as Knifer sliced the head off one skeletal zombie and sliced backhand at the neck of another.

There were several shots behind them as Greg and one of Knifer's friends dispatched the undead who had been pushed down by the tractor's plough. As the echoes subsided and the partial deafness from the firing began receding, he took Sam's arm, there was a little blood, but only a minor wound. She looked at his hand, at him and snatched her arm back.

'Sam,' he said, then as her eyes took on a unfocussed gaze he shouted her name within inches of her face.

'Wha?' she slurred, her mouth still gasping at air.

'C'mon' you need a drink.'

He took her by the hand and pulled her back towards the bus.

'Greg, have you got a sugary drink and some sweets. She needs it now, as do we all.'

For all Greg's ineptness with the gun and his momentary hesitation the man was a good organiser. Within a minute he was passing around cans of cola and a number of large bags of sugar-covered gummy sweets. Sam gulped at her can.

'Tom brought those for the children,' she said. Greg replied there was plenty for everyone.

For Carragher he fought back the trembling but could only slump to the ground as his legs shook. He took what he thought what was a can of cola, until he swallowed a mouthful of lukewarm lager. Knifer smiled, in a you needed that grin, as he tipped his own can into his mouth, and pulled a hipflask from his baggy jacket and handed it over. The major took a large swig and handed it back. He knew that he had to take charge here as the chaos would present an opportunity for more vigilantes or zombies to converge.

He stood, looked at Knifer in the eyes.

'How many civilians dead? And how many of your friends?'

'Too many. Big Joe took shrapnel to the side of the head, Suzanne, well she bled out. Billy is okay, and he can still fight even with the amount of cuts and bruises he has accumulated over the last eight days.

'Not sure about the civilians. The police man for sure. You're lot?'

He gestured with a nod of his head towards the blown-up vehicle, and the one flipped on its side by the blast.

'At least 10 soldiers, and five police dead. Not sure about injuries.'

CHAPTER 13

Jude was using the plough on the tractor to shovel bodies of the undead over the edge of a small hill. Revulsion was deep on his face, and the shakes that followed any battle. Sam was experiencing the same shakes. The sugar rush abated some of it, but her thoughts were dominated by worrying about post-traumatic stress disorder. She was sure she would experience it at some point, but she was concerned at the impact on the children. They had experienced enough already, and then this. Watching their de facto guardian Tom take his own life, would scar them. He had been their big cuddly uncle who made them laugh, and now some had seen him bitten by a zombie and put his handgun to his head to save himself from infection.

Greg walked towards her, seeing her standing upright, but somehow slumped in her demeanour.

He put a hand on her shoulder, felt the initial flinch then she turned and hugged him hard. He returned the hug and said into her ear, 'we need to get ourselves organised.'

She pulled back, rubbed her eyes hard, and gave him a half smile.

Looking towards the carnage of the army and police vehicles. The police inspector was marching two of the vigilantes towards Carragher and Knifer. Knifer gestured for them to join them. Trying to keep her eyes from looking at the mutilated flesh around the vehicles, she and Greg walked, both straining themselves to remain steady.

'Well, what should we do with these?' said Knifer.

Sam looked at the two men. They had the look she had seen of prisoners from the world war documentaries her father watched endlessly when he was drunk, with loud music playing at the same time. It was a look of fear as to what they would face, an undercurrent of self-anger at being defeated, and hope the risk of death was now gone.

'Inspector,' she said. 'You would seem to be the most senior civil authority here.'

Carragher intimated that he had already said that, but before anyone could respond Knifer punched both men. It was so quick not one person could react.

'I do believe that is in breach of the Geneva Convention,' said Carragher, his voice laced with a mixture of sarcasm and indifference.

'The Geneva Convention has been suspended for the time being.'

Bryson, glanced towards the two vigilantes. Greg thought she looked like she would like an hour alone with them in a holding cell with a baton in her hand.

'Inspector,' began Greg, 'Wait, she interrupted, you can call me Samantha.'

"For fuck sake, don't tell Smicker or we will never hear the end of it," Sam cut in. The inspector recognised this as some sort of in joke and ignored it.

'We will need to search them, then ask some questions,' said the police officer.

Carragher gestured to two soldiers making sure they knew to look for bladed weapons and drugs.

'Dump any drugs you find on the road, apart from amphetamines,' Carragher said. A questioning look from a corporal was greeted with the arched eyebrows only an officer can pull that says just do as your told.

The search did produce one knife, two bags of cannabis, some anonymous white powder they claimed was cocaine and three bags of tablets they said were 'speed'.

Questioning took less than a minute with Knifer standing over them, and Greg, Sam and Carragher flanking Bryson. Confirmation that they had no radio, confirmation that there may be more KKK in the area, but not close, and that they were shit scared.

Carragher asked Bryson to move aside.

'Right, given you have attacked police officers, attacked soldiers and endangered civilians, injuring some and killing several, ordinarily you would be detained awaiting trial. As we have no holding cells, no solicitor to represent you, and no court room I am going to offer you a choice.

"You can be cuffed here to the Land Rover you blew up awaiting us to find a solicitor to represent you, or you can take a shitload of the amphetamines and run back down the road?'

Knifer stepped forward again, grabbed one by the lower jaw and forced the alleged amphetamines into his mouth, and repeated the same with the second man. Delivering a punch to each man's head as they swallowed, he said. 'It appears they have made u their mind'.

A police officer was already uncuffing them and Sam began, given the situation, what was to be a speech.

'If you, or any of your colleagues, decide to follow us, or attack us again they will be met with extreme prejudice. An attack on military, police or civilians justifies deadly force, as the inspector here will confirm,' she said, continuing before Bryson could respond.

'Should you run into any more of your friends you tell them they are not to interfere with us, or they will be killed. You are nothing to us. Now go!'

They turned and began to run, but not quick enough to avoid a comical boot in the ass for one of them from Knifer. Stumbling he set off as if in an Olympic sprint final.

CHAPTER 14

Brady and everyone had heard the gunfire in the distant, and all turned to the sound of the explosion.

"Eyes on the prize gentlemen,' he said. 'We will slow down and prepare for what will be a difficult task.

'To explain, once we fire the on the frigate we will approach the rear of the frigate. There are a number of points there we can use to board. We are facing, from what I have been given to believe will be some Icelandic fishermen, and some Royal Navy traitors.

'These men have betrayed the oath they took to the Crown, the oath they took to their friends serving as their comrades in uniform. Under the authority of the current governing body if they do not surrender, they are to be met with deadly force. I know this is unpleasant, but it is necessary. As for the Icelandic aboard, they are to be regarded as enemy combatants.

'Now I believe it would be opportune to eat the shit rations you have and take a wee tot of rum.'

Allen produced the two bottles of rum from his bergen and passed the first bottle around.

Brady sat down, still fuming at Carragher's defiance, and a nagging sense of the futileness of this mission. Still, he mused, he had been on futile missions before that had succeeded despite the odds, mainly due to his stubbornness and that of soldiers willing to obey orders.

Allen offered him the bottle of rum, but he shook his head. He lit a cigarette and gazed out to sea to compose himself. He had drunk enough over the past week and needed a clear head. Too old for this shit, he thought, but orders were orders.

Although it was framed as a request Brady's experience

told him that if he was to have any credibility when this shit show finally ended, and have a position, not necessarily of power but of influence, he had to try. He had nothing else to live for anyway.

Beckoning Allen over he told him what he was planning.

'I know you have your doubts sergeant about what we are doing, and I too have reservations,' he said in what for him was a quiet reserved tone. 'This isn't just about orders. There is a bigger agenda that I cannot tell anyone just yet, but I will explain closer to the time.'

Allen nodded, with a slight tip of his head, a motion he knew from experience that officers of all ranks responded to. Brady took the cue.

'Seizing this frigate isn't just a matter of pride for the armed forces,' he said. Some might say It could even be perceived that it is something to do with Brittania ruling the waves, or some such shit. But that is not the case.

'The truth is I'm not sure we can do it, but we must try. I promise you that I will do everything to not endanger any of our lives, if at all possible.'

Allen noted that qualification in the statement but simply said, "yes sir".

Allen was watching the general's body language. The flicking of the ash from his cigarette when it didn't need tapping, and was almost out, the slight shifting of the shoulders, the small glances to the left. It told him Brady was a lying bastard.

Chapter 15

Three minibuses, a Land Rover and a tractor pulled away from site where there had been so many casualties. Greg had been insistent that there was not time to bury the bodies, but some had insisted on covering them. His instinct was that the gunfire and explosion would attract unwanted attention whether it was from vigilantes or zombies. He was also conscious of the time still needed to reach Ballycastle.

Also, he was conscious that getting moving would give them a purpose to avoid thinking of what had happened.

He and Sam had a brief conversation about whether to tell the soldiers, police and Knifer about Iceland. Carragher knew but had said nothing. After the soldiers blocked the windows of the minibuses with bergens Sam indicated she would speak with them, just simply saying that they had a right to know.

She joined Carragher, Knifer and Bryson in the Land Rover as they got underway.

Two soldiers and a police officer were with them in the back, another man at the wheel.

'Look, some might already know this, but we are going to Ballycastle to meet with representatives of the Icelandic government,' she said. 'We have been offered refuge there. They are free from infection, but they need hands to help sustain themselves with no imports allowed.

'They also fear that there may be attempts, from those less welcome, to land and would seize control. They are offering unconditional sanctuary until such times as this epidemic has passed. All who flee there are free to leave at any time.'

She looked around. They were glancing at each other. Bryson was the first to speak.

'I'm staying, but anyone who has been under my command is free to make their own decision. My reasons for staying are complicated, but let's just say there needs to be some semblance of law and order as we go forward.'

Carragher said: "I may have the rank of major but after telling the general to fuck off I believe I may no longer hold that rank, so I will not ask anyone present to stay or go. I will go, if they will have me.'

'I'll go," Knifer said. "Always wanted to see a volcano anyway.'

There was nervous laughter, until one of the soldiers said he would stay, the other indicated he would go. The remaining police officer looked at Bryson and said he would like to go.

Sam knew she would have liked to give them more time. She tapped the soldier at the wheel on the shoulder.

'Can you pull next to the minibuses so I can make the same offer and contact our other group?' she said. 'What about you?'

He laughed, and in a broad Scouse accent said: 'Send me on my way to sunny Iceland, love,'

Five minutes later she was talking to Smicker on board the leading minibus. She noted that the soldiers had placed bits of panelling from the wrecked vehicles on broken windows and placed begems against the rest, as she spoke.

'How close are you to Ballycastle?'

She could hear the sound of distant explosions.

'Well, we're pretty close, a bit too fucking close,' he said. "Our Icelandic and navy friends have a big grey navy ship and are blowing the shit out of any zombies.

'We ended up going along the coast on account of some bastards shooting at us, but Seamus drove like a mad cunt and Jenny shot back.

We've just passed Bushmills, got you a few bottles to break the ice with the Icelandic, and get blind fucking drunk. But yeah, we're close enough."

'We're about an hour out, maybe less," she replied. 'We have some additional people, soldiers and police, who would like to go. Can you ask them when you are in contact next.'

'I'll be telling them to use that fucking gun a bit more carefully first, but I don't think there would be a problem.

'And you'll never believe who is organising the boarding? Another north Belfast cunt. Called Malachy, he was on holiday in Iceland and decided to lend a hand and translate. Apparently, our accent is difficult to understand.'

As usual Smicker was making light of his stress and the situation. But she knew he was referring to the whiskey and north Belfast craic to keep away the severity of this final dash.

After the conversation she asked Greg about the best way to keep going forward.

'I think we keep at no more than 20 miles per hour,' he said. 'That way we are keeping good enough speed, and we will be slow enough to be prepared for any surprises.'

She nodded and looked at the children. As she looked, she was amazed that the soldiers, the highly trained killers, were taking the time to chat to them. One was passing around bits of chocolate, another was enquiring about one girl's doll. She was about 12, too old for a doll but it gave her become a comfort amidst the stress.

As she looked forward there came a feeling of tremors racing up and down her body, and for a second she thought she would collapse, until she saw Jude gesturing from the tractor.

Ahead, about 500 yards away, was another group of zombies. Maybe 10 or 15 were stumbling along the road. She knew after their last encounter there could be more lining the road. Fron somewhere she gathered the strength to speak.

'Jude, go as fast as you can,' she shouted into the radio. 'Elijah, keep up, Greg pass it on to the rest we're speeding up.'

She gestured to two of the soldiers. 'Get your weapons ready any that try to grab on, or look like they might attempt to, shoot. Pass the same message to all behind us.'

Jude pushed the tractor faster and in seconds the first zombies were pushed aside by the plough. One decapitated head flew airborne with the impact and Elijah swore as it bounced off the windscreen. The minibus shuddered as it ran over an undead body, and she watched as the soldiers fired with controlled bursts to the side.

The tractor came to a sudden halt, the engine was revving, but there was something stopping it.

Jude turned, eyes wide, as one of the undead was crawling up the side of the tractor.

'I hit a motorbike, and the plough is trapped on it and the bodies, he said. 'I didn't see it. What the fuck can I do, fucking help, help me, they'll get in. Jesus fucking Christ I'm fucking going to die.'

'Hold tight," Carragher said, with a calmness belying the situation. 'We will come alongside, and we'll try to push you over it, and clear the zombies off.'

The Land Rover rammed the back of the tractor, and it did not move. One of the soldiers came out of the back and fired twice at the zombie clambering up the tractor cab. The bullets passed through the skeletal frame, not altering its clawing at the door. He walked closer and sent a round through the side of its skull and it slid off the vehicle. He glanced around and seeing the zombies nearby ran back to the safety of his vehicle, slamming the door.

Sam's body was shaking, yet her thoughts were clear. She shouted to try again while measuring in her head how much time Jude would need to reach safety if he ran. It would be less than 10 seconds before one of the scrambling undead got into the cab.

The Land Rover surged forward, juddered as it hit the tractor. For a second it seemed just to be jammed, then the plough jumped up halfway and the spinning rear wheels gripped, and it surged forward. One zombie still clung on as others fell off. Jude fumbled with his pistol, trying to hold on to the wheel at the same time. It took three shots before one hit the head and it fell off.

Go, go, go,' Sam shouted and as it moved the vehicles followed, too fast for any zombies to grab on to.

‘Fuck me,’ said Greg.

‘Yeah, fuck you old man,’ replied Sam. ‘Just get everyone on alert.’

CHAPTER 16

Smicker was nibbling his nails, something he hadn't done since a child. His mother always told him off until the nagging finally paid off. Now his nerves drew his fingers to his mouth. Despite all his banter and shitty sarcasm, he was now terrified. The reality that he might be signing his own death certificate by agreeing to stay behind swam over his mind. The race to reach Ballycastle had kept it occupied. Jenny's steady leadership and ferocity had kept all steady, not least him. Sure, having Seamus and Greg would be great in some band of brothers shit, but Sam and Jenny were their heartbeat.

He tore his fingers away from his mouth and looked around. Jenny was lining up the vehicles and Seamus was finishing up with his improvised mine field. It never ceased to amaze Smicker that meticulous tasks came to the marine so easily. He was almost casual as he filled pipes with gunpowder, added some sort of shit Smicker didn't understand then buried them a few inches deep into the soil.

'Right, that's that done,' Seamus said. 'Jenny you can get us ready to roll now, I'll put up another sign lest the unwary tread here. Smicker, do you think zombies can read?'

'Fuck I can barely read never mind the zombies.'

The pair ran with an easy gait towards the vehicles, falling in step together. As they jumped on the first bus. They were about to start moving when the radio crackled.

'Hi there, it's Malachy here. Thon big ship tells us that despite shelling the fuck out of the perimeter and everything else they think that from they can see from the drone some of them soldiers and a clatter of the undead coming your way too.'

'Well fuck me pink and dip me in sherbert that's just another piece on fun for us," said Smicker. 'Sure, what do you want us to do Malachy take all the fun and games you and the Vikings can't handle.'

'Nah, we've enough fun underway here. The woman shooting the big gun wants you to try and direct fire for her when you have visuals. Any of you know how to do it.'

They looked at Seamus, who was already tweaking his device and scanning a map.

'Aye, we have a geek Royal Marine who can do that. We'll give you a shout when he is finished folding his map.'

Seamus without looking raised his middle finger to Smicker. Jenny sighed. 'You know sometimes I wish you two eejits had went with Sam," she said. 'Seeing as I'm still stuck with you, now can you just shut the fuck up Smicker for 30 seconds.'

Smicker just blew her a kiss and walked down the bus checking on weapons and the children. He was worried about them. But he was also thinking about the future. How many other children were out there on their own. He could only hope of his personal salvation by saving as many as he could.

Then a massive explosion 200 yards away from him. No point in ducking but he did anyway.

'Fuck sake Seamus, get them to be more careful, near shit myself.'

The marine was on the radio, hopefully helping the gunner improve their targeting.

Jenny was standing on the bonnet of the lead vehicle she was scanning the horizon with a pair of binoculars. To Smicker she epitomised the image of a warrior queen amidst the chaos. Like Sam she had a presence he couldn't define. As a 40-something asshole he wished he had met either of them when he was younger, when he hadn't made as many mistakes.

He had no faith and was never one to sit in the pews apart from funerals and weddings, but he had discovered his conscience; and whatever part of his emerging moral code again he swore to himself he would seek redemption by saving as many people as he could.

Another explosion, but this sounded different, even closer.

Jenny jumped off the vehicle and Seamus shouted.

'Mortar, mortar, get down.'

Jenny took a deep breath. 'So, what do we do about that.' Seamus looked around, scanning the people around him.

'Jenny stay with the rest get them undercover, Smicker, with me, we'll try to out flank it.'

Moving towards where the sound came from Seamus gestured to two others.

'You three move to the right, move forward, get in cover and fire in the general direction of where you think it is, I'll go around as close as I can.'

'Aye, so you want them to shoot as us. Fuck Seamus what's your next big idea?'

'If you've got a better idea, fire away.'

'Nah, I'm all out of petrol bombs so it's up to you.'

Chapter 17

'Captain please feel free to advance the fastest you can go,' said Brad to the grizzled old man at the wheel. 'Corporal, prepare the TOW to fire.'

The frigate was, Allen estimated, about 700 yards away, anchored to the north of Rathlin Island. Close enough for the TOW but maybe it needed to be a bit closer to be reliable.

The radio crackled.

'To the little boat approaching us, please turn away,' a heavily accented voice said.

Brady grabbed the mic: 'This is Geneal Brady commander of British forces in Northern Ireland. I am ordering you to surrender the vessel to Crown Forces.'

'And, I am Captain Viking, and you General can fuck away off, and fuck off in your little boat.'

'This is your last chance to surrender.'

The connection ended, but Allen swore he could hear laughter before it ended.

'Corporal, fire at will.'

Resting on top of the cabin, the weapon prepared, he fired. Allen watched the missile streak towards the ship. It had gotten less than halfway when a burst of fire erupted from the frigate and the missile disintegrated in a grey cloud.

'"Phalanx gatling gun," said Allen out loud. Radar guided, could take us all in another burst.'

Brady didn't seem at all flustered.

'Nevertheless, we will seize this frigate, Captain, please navigate to the rear of the frigate. And what you might not know yet, is that 100 soldiers from Londonderry are now advancing on Ballycastle to make sure that those trying to escape have no hope.'

As he spoke a shot flaked wood from the bow. Another

clipped the starboard rail. Then the tiny radio mast was blown away. Allen focussed on the frigate. There were three men, barely visible, training high powered rifles on the boat.

'Special forces, SBS,' he thought to himself. 'If they really had wanted to hit us we'd be all dead.'

Turning to the stern Allen pulled off his boots, threw down his webbing, rifle and ammo, wrapped the pistol he'd been carrying in plastic and was about to jump overboard when Brady bellowed.

'What the fuck are doing sergeant.'

'Getting the hell off before they get serious on that frigate, that shooting wasn't just grunts laying down fire.'

'Insubordination and desertion, you'll face a firing squad if I don't shoot you on this boat,' the general said, his face reddening in anger.

'Aye, dead on you daft cunt,' Allen said before taking two steps and diving off the boat. He took three strokes underwater, before surfacing. He expected to see the general taking aim, but instead he saw most of the other soldiers getting ready to dive over. Brady was fuming at them, but one by one they began to reach the water. Even at the distance he could see the general's face bright red.

Rathlin Island was about 300 yards away. He was fit, but was he fit enough? He trod water for a moment before committing to a flailing front crawl. He had managed about 10 strokes when he heard more shooting. He paused and saw that the boat's hull had been hit several times, the engine was sputtering, and it was listing to starboard. He didn't wait to see what Brady and the rest were going to do, he just kept swimming. His uniform was dragging but he kept going.

CHAPTER 18

'What the fuck was that?' said Sam as they heard the explosion from the water.

'I think that was the general's attempt to damage the frigate failing miserably,' said Greg.

'Right, enough, we need to organise all of us. Elijah, get Jenny, Seamus and Smicker on the radio. Jude, keep us moving slowly. Carragher and Byson, please join us.'

A moment later Jenny's voice came through.

'What's up with you lot?

Sam cut in.

'We are less than 20 minutes out from Ballycastle if we don't meet anymore shit shows. What's your situation?

'We have been pinned down by some soldiers. We were under what Seamus said was mortar fire. He and Smicker went off with a few others to try and sort it out. They seem to have succeeded. No more interruptions we should be at the Icelandic perimeter in 10 minutes.'

'Okay, we'll try and catch you up.'

'Just be careful, I think that some of the soldiers that were firing are trying to outflank us, and that's what the mortar fire might have been for. Oh, and watch out for minefield.'

Greg spoke, 'Minefield?'

'Hello Greg, yes minefield. Seamus made up some pipe bombs when we were on our way. He rigged some with fuses he said would explode if you walked on them. Don't know how, don't need to know, but the area they are planted in is marked and he said the tractor's plough would dig most of them up if you need to cross it. Right, got to go. See ya soon.'

'Bye' said Sam before turning to the rest of them. 'We press on. Inspector, if you want to turn back, or any of those who are staying want to turn back, do so now.'

'No thank you Sam. If there are civilians in the area not caught up in this mess, we can help.'

Sam nodded to Greg and the rest of those around.'

'Okay, let's all go to the seaside. Candy floss, ice cream and greasy chips.'

CHAPTER 19

Allen was tiring, he felt his strokes slowing and every other stroke he ended up swallowing sea water. He paused, treading water as the small waves rippled on his stubbled chin. He saw one of the swimmers come level.

'Sargeant, you may want to look over your shoulder.'

Less than 10 yards away were two inflatable boats, there motors slowly edging them closer to the small group of swimmers. Strong hands reached out, hauling Allen and others on board.

Allen was still gasping when he saw the boat they had arrived in slide beneath the waves. He saw Brady, the captain and three others cling to bits of wood.

'What about them?' he said to the man at the outboard motor. His only reply was they would have to wait.

Less than five minutes later he was ashore facing a man and woman who were pointing shotguns at them.

'The woman spoke: 'I hope you are not planning anything like taking over the island, because that isn't going to happen. There are some very nice Icelandic fellas over there, and they brought us some tinned fish and bottles of drink. I don't think they'd be the sort of people you would want to annoy.'

Allen looked at the two. 'You will get no trouble from us, I think I can speak for all of us that we have had enough but right now I could do some damage to a cup of tea.'

He looked out to sea and saw the two inflatables heading towards Brady and the others.

'As to that man who says he is a general, don't believe a word he says. I did, and found out he doesn't care about anyone even those he is commanding. Your Icelandic friends might want to know he was the one that ordered the missile to be fired.'

'Don't worry, I think they know.'

'Let's get you a cuppa, then you can talk to them yourself'

He and the other soaked men walked in front of the pair, but at least they had lowered the shotguns. Shortly they were sitting outside a house, and an elderly man was pouring tea from a large, ancient tea pot. Allen mumbled a thank you and sipped the tea. It's heat and sweetness restorative. A shadow passed in front of him. A bear of a man towered over him, bearded and with broad shoulders and biceps that spoke of native strength. Beside him a small woman stood, legs shoulder width apart and hand on a large knife. Allen thought that he could try to fight the man, but this woman would happily carve him open before he could lay a blow.

'My name is Inge, and this is Bjorn. Who is in charge here?"

Allen looked at the men with him. They were all looking at him.

'I was a sergeant, but I have resigned from the army from the moment I dived off that boat. But I can speak for us all I think.' He turned to the bedraggled bunch he came ashore with, and they nodded.

'Right,' said Inge. 'We are going to Ballycastle in five minutes. We have space for you all. When you get there, you will have two choices. One is to stay there. The second is to join us in Iceland. Make up your mind when we launch.'

'Thank you M'am. And to everyone who helped us we thank you. And, for the tea.'

Moments later he was on a trawler. Watching Bjorn drag Brady by the collar on board, and Inge holding he knife to his throat.

'You tried to kill my friends, I'll let them decide what to do with you, you fifl.'

Allen wasn't sure what that word was, but the venom in Inge's voice made him think she wasn't being complimentary.

Chapter 20

Jude looked enormous in the cab of the tactor, wearing soldier's body armour, helmet and body armour over his legs. Another layer was around the footwell of the cab. Sam was surprised the young man had volunteered. He had seen so much like them all, but the tractor had been where he had nearly been taken by zombies. Yet, she hadn't needed to ask for volunteers. He stepped forward and asked the soldiers that if he was going to drive the tractor could he borrow some body armour.

She reckoned Smicker was the one who had written the signs marking the minefield. The road ahead was blocked with rubble and the other side was choked with trees and thick scrub. And, in front of the minefield were the two signs reading: 'Do not cross, here be things that go boom'.

After getting the vehicles in line in the field Jude lowered the snow plough head until it was grazing the top of the soil. He repeated what he had said several times, 'stay in a straight line behind me.'

All the engines came to life and were bumping along slowly over the field. Sam thought she could see the slight disturbances in the grass where the mines could be, but this was a better way to try and cross it than sheer guess work.

The soldiers were chatting away to the children, and one was explaining to JoJo that he shouldn't try using a rifle but in time he would show him how to use a pistol. Elijah opened a can of coke, and the pop made everyone look up.

They were just over halfway across when there was an explosion. Bits of soil and small stones fell on the minibus, and the tractor was obscured in smoke and a dust cloud.

Shouting Sam called Jude's name three times, her hand on the radio mic gripped so tight Greg could see her knuckles whiten.

'Aye, aye I'm okay. Think I might have pissed myself.'

Sam exhaled deeply. Greg clapped her gently on the back.

'Can you see if there is any damage to the rear tires? I think one if the front ones might be burst.'

When the smoke cleared, they confirmed that there was no visible damage.

'Okay, there's some smoke coming from the engine, I don't know how much longer it will last, so I'm going to risk going a bit faster.'

Without waiting for a reply, he pushed onwards, and they all followed.

When the tractor reached the field boundary another explosion and the rear of the tractor buckled down, its large rear wheels splayed outwards.

Before she could reach for the radio, Jude stumbled out of the cab, blood flowing from his left arm. He motioned them forward and began tossing pieces of body armour on the ground. It was clear that he was saying this was the only path they could take, and Elijah pushed on, giving Jude a thumbs up as they passed.

The vehicles crossed the final small ditch and Jude stepped forward and collapsed.

CHAPTER 21

Seamus was in a small ditch he had seen the three soldiers at the mortar, he did not want to shoot any of them, but they were trying to kill his friends. Until a few weeks ago he didn't know he could feel such a bond outside of a few he trained with. But he regarded this group of survivors as true friends. Mad, bad and sometimes wonderful.

He watched as the soldiers responded to the gunfire from Smicker's group. They abandoned the mortar to seek cover. At just over 100 feet away he fired short bursts into the mortar tube. They passed through and rendered it useless. The group looked around to where this second fusillade had come from. Seamus stood up.

'Cease fire Smicker," he said. 'I'm sorry you three but please lay down your arms, you are covered from two sides, and I have seen too much killing as it is.'

They looked confused, but one by one set their weapons down. Seamus walked towards them, as did Smicker and the two who had accompanied him. The soldiers were surprised when he extended his hand to shake each of theirs. Smicker just laughed and said: 'Fancy a wee trip to Iceland?

'It's either that or stay with some mad bastards killing zombies and saving civilians. Anyway, just walk this way.'

Seamus made clear they could pick up their rifles, but the magazine should be removed until they made up their mind.

Walking back towards where Jenny was Smicker said he would follow, as he had a 'sortta call of nature, like.'

Seamus grunted and walked on. Call of nature my arse, he thought knowing Smicker was likely to be drinking, smoking some weed, or generally getting up to mischief.

Just over five minutes later Jenny was chatting to the drivers about how they were to approach the Icelandic perimeter when a look out shouting: zombies. To their south a swarm of about 30 zombies were stumbling through a field. Behind them a loud engine roared, and an armoured personnel carrier drove straight at the zombies.

It ran them down like a runaway combine harvester in a field of rabbits. Poking his head through the hatch was Smicker. 'Yeeeoooo, he shouted.'

The zombies that were left were quickly dispatched before the vehicle stopped.

The door opened and Smicker jumped out and said to the driver, 'See, I told you that would be fun.'

Seamus and Jenny looked at Smicker, the Warrior APC, and back at Smicker. In unison they said: 'What the fuck?'

Smicker grinned.

'I'm from north Belfast. I fucking hijacked it. These two were having a wee cup of tea and a smoke and I convinced them with a gun and a joint that they were better with us.'

Jenny sighed, Seamus mumbled under his breath 'mad fucker' and the two soldiers begged another joint from Smicker.

'Right,' Jenny said. 'Time to move out.'

'Before we do, we should warn Sam; these two reckon there are about 30 of their friends coming to where she is.'

CHAPTER 22

'So, what's your story?" Sam said. Knifer was gazing towards the sea. His side profile caught the sunlight, its glare hiding his features. When he turned towards Sam, she saw that with his stubble and slightly ruffled hair he could pass for a hipster after a night out drinking over-priced beer, except for his eyes.

You could read pain, in them, a sadness that spoke of experiences that were carved into his soul.

'What do you want to know?'

'How did get the name Knifer?'

"Well, that is one long fucking story, but let's just say for now my childhood memories are of dog shit and despair, and I started carrying a knife to school when I was 13. If I get to a volcano in Iceland, I'll tell you everything. "

"Fair enough," Sam said. "Right now, I want to get the children on to boats before it's too late, I don't feel comfortable waiting here, and when they are moving the children won't think too much about what they have been through.

"Yep, me too, I don't like being lunch for a zombie or have some trigger-happy cunt open up."

With barely a pause he put his rifle to his shoulder, Sam saw a zombie with no legs pulling itself along on its elbows. One shot, its head, parted in the middle, grey gook oozed out of its rotten jaw.

"If you kill something that is already dead, is it still killing," Knifer said.

Sam looked away. He had shot the zombie 200 feet away and chatted away like a hairdresser trimming as she worked. This was a calm professionalism that spoke of extreme training and hard experience.

"Err, I guess we can only fight them until we can't fight anymore. We'll define it later."

Knifer looked at her. "Fight them until we can't fight anymore. I like it, sort of Rourkes Drift."

"Sort of paraphrased that from a thrash metal song."

"You'll have to play that for me, but right now Sam the shit is about to hit the fan."

Sam turned and saw three soldiers crouch, rifles to their shoulders, Carragher shouted, "Knifer, your three o'clock".

Knifer grabbed Sam by her shoulder and pushed her down. He handed her a pistol, and shouted to his two companions, "flank right".

Facing them were at least 25 soldiers. Knifer nodded to Carragher with a tilt of his head to the left, and Sam watched as the man edged to the left.

"On the orders of General Brady, you are to lay down your arms, all uniformed combatants, are to surrender to military authority, civilians to assemble peacefully, and offer no protest."

Sam heard Knifer cock his rifle. She stood up, pushing it gently down.

All 25 rifles were now trained on her.

"May I ask your name, and your rank?

The soldier who spoke looked straight at her he paused. Here, to him, was just a young girl, but she spoke in calm tones that suggested to him leadership.

He paused then said; 'Lieutenant John Taylor, 2 RIR. I am here at the command of General Brady to detain any personages attempting to reach Ballycastle or beyond and believe me we will carry out his orders.'

'Personages,' said Sam. 'You mean people, people still living, as opposed to the undead. You mean people that bleed when they are shot, people that scream, cry and sob from wounds. Are those the type of people you aim to prevent reaching a nice wee seaside town?'

When the Lieutenant responded saying yes. Sam replied

with a bitter tone in her voice: 'I have seen friends die, I've seen them being eaten by zombies, I've seen children die, and if you try to prevent us moving forward you will shed more blood, you may even kill children. Are those the orders you want to carry out? Carragher, Knifer if you will.'

The two men dropped to a crouch and fired two bullets each. Sam had no idea what they would do but trusted her instincts. Two hit the ground in front of each of the lieutenant's feet, the same at the feet of the man beside him.

She was expecting fire in response, but beside her now stood Jude, holding the general-purpose machine gun.

'These boys are accurate, but I don't need to be with this.'

Sam saw that Jude was swaying. There was blood oozing from the crude bandage on his wound. She took the heavy gun from him and turned to the soldiers facing them.

'Look, pay attention to this. I don't give a fuck about your orders. I don't give a fuck who gave them. I am going to get these people and all these children to Ballycastle. So, please lower your weapons and. Stand. At. Fucking. Ease'

Wow was all Knifer said in response to the roar from Sam.

Taylor turned to the man beside him, who just shrugged and lowered his rifle. Carragher recognised the wisdom of an inexperienced officer relying on an NCO.

Greg just came forward with beers to hand round.

Sam heard the radio crackle, then Smicker came on the line: 'Just wanted t give you a heads up you might get some military company coming your way.'

'Bit fucking late, We're on our way now.'

'Okay, give five minutes I'll be there.'

CHAPTER 23

Jenny saw Smicker smile, and say he 'off to see Sam, for a bit of craic.' She sighed and said she would see hm at the perimeter as soon as he stopped playing with his new toy.

The Warrior vehicle's tracks threw clumps of mud in the air as the by now stoned driver headed off. It was to be a final effort to reach the perimeter the Icelandic team had created for safe embarkation on to the awaiting boats. She called to Seamus.

'We need to get the vehicles organised. They are too strung out. Can we cram more into a couple of them," she said to the Royal Marine. 'When we reach that perimeter, I want us through it as quickly as possible, and on to those boats.'

Seamus thought that Jenny had grown and truly become a leader as well as the warrior she had already been, She set out the aim and asked those around her the best way to achieve that aim. He suspected that within six months Sam and her would be in charge of half of Iceland.

'Best way would be to reduce the number of vehicles to three, and as that is being done, and everyone crammed in I'll take a quick recce through the streets leading to the harbour, and report back in five minutes.

'Then, if everything is clear and doable we proceed at slowly, unless we see a reason to speed up.'

'Okay Seamus, make it so.'

She caught herself saying those three words, she was a Trekkie and from her unconsciousness she had dragged up a line from Captain Picard. Seamus didn't seem to notice as he walked away, but for her it was a memory of her family settled down watching their favourite sci fi shows. It made her more determined to keep the children and frightened civilians safe.

One of the young teenage children was sipping a can of

cola, just about to get on board. He turned to her.

'Jenny, I really need to piss. I'm bursting.'

She laughed.

'Aye, so am I. Tell you what, go round the back of that last minibus, I'll go with you, but I promise not to peek.'

Satisfied that the vehicles were almost filled, she walked to a now empty minibus.

She could hear the steady stream from the boy's bladder, then a trembling quiet voice.

'J J J Jenny, can you help me.'

She rounded the back to see the boy staring at a zombie that was mere feet away from him. Not knowing it but she took in the time it would take this shuffling creature to reach the lad, what her options were, all in less than a second.

She ran the two metres to the boy, pushed him behind her, lifted her rifle and fired twice into the shambling mess. It staggered, but she had missed the head. She swept its legs it fell on to its side, she launched a kick into its midriff and pulled a knife, driving it into the creature's eye.

Behind her the boy said, 'I think I've pissed on my trousers.'

She ginned. 'Well, I think I pissed myself too John. C'mon we should get back to the bus.'

As they boarded, she checked how everyone has squeezed in, not happy with the way they were randomly sitting and standing.

'Children in the middle. C'mon people, think. Adults sitting by the windows, children sitting by the aisle, rest standing.' She pointed at the three men 'captured' by Seamus. 'Tell your colleagues back there, if they aren't too stoned, they are to ride in the door wells. And, if you try to fuck us over, I will gladly put two rounds in the back.'

Seamus, back from his reconnaissance, walking forward to the lead vehicle, told them that she would and not lose a single minute's sleep.

'We're going down the street on the right, then 100 yards

after that turn left and the perimeter is 500 yards away. I'll radio Malachy when we make that turn.'

CHAPTER 24

As the soldiers in front of them shuffled, faced by the machine gun, Sam wanted to find out more about them, in case they were needed, and to see how loyal they were to Brady.

As she was about to begin the conversation there was sound of a diesel engine, coming closer. The lieutenant smiled and lifted his rifle, pointing it at Sam. She didn't flinch but began to worry when she saw the armoured vehicle approach, its tracks smashing through a low hedge.

The lieutenant's smile grew wider. 'It seems the tables have turned young lady, and I hold the aces now.'

Sam looked over his shoulder and burst out laughing. 'Oh, no,' she said, struggling to speak through growing laughter. Greg just said, 'ach fer fuck sake I might have known.

The lieutenant turned to look. The Warrior drew to a stop and sitting on top of its canon was Smicker, bottle of whiskey in hand, and cigarette in mouth.

'Yeeooo, the fucking cavalry is here, fucked up and ready to fuck people up. Hey pretty boy,' he said, pointing to the lieutenant. 'I suggest you put that gun down, before you get hurt.'

Sam could see the confusion in the lieutenant' eyes, captured, redemption hoped for, and now this. He looked around at the men he had been with. Some had already slumped to the ground, others were standing with rifles pointing towards her group, others towards Smicker and his hijacked armoured personnel carrier.

She sensed a movement in the lieutenant's hand and before she could register it a knife was sticking into the back of it.

Knifer had another blade in his hand. 'Next one goes in your throat pretty boy.'

Addressing the soldiers, not the lieutenant, Sam said they need not head towards more killing and there would be a chance to do some good.

'When we get to Ballycastle there are boats waiting to take us to Iceland. If you wish some of you can come, others can stay, report to Greg and work through the country to rescue and support civilians and try to begin to build some sort of order. Think about it.'

Carrgher yelled her name, when she turned Jude had fallen and his face had turned a worryingly grey. She tossed the heavy machine gun to the ground.

'Knifer, find out if any of them eejits has a more than basic first aid kit, or if there is one in thon thing Smicker nicked. Greg, use the machine gun to keep an eye on the lot of them.'

Kneeling down she saw the grass was soaked in blood. The bandage on his arm was blood soaked, and Jude was holding his stomach. Knifer threw a green box with a red cross on it to the ground as Sam was about to lift the bandage.

'Hold, on, don't do that,'' he said. Speaking very gently he said to Jude, 'are your guts sore Buddy? I'm going to lift your shirt for a second, I'll be gentle.'

Jude nodded, and as Knifer lifted his shirt Sam saw that it was distended and grey, with veins standing out. Knifer touched the side of the swollen stomach.

He turned to Sam and shook his head.

'Mate, you're going to need something for the pain. Is that okay?'

He took something from the first aid box and out of Sam's site line, injected two vials into the young man's arm. He reached into his pouch and pulled out a hip flask. He muttered something about taking the taste away and held it to Jude's blue lips.

Setting the hip flask down he injected two more vials. He reached forward, and closed Jude's eyes.

Sitting back, he said, 'Internal bleeding, probably a ruptured spleen, maybe a punctured bowel. He must have gotten it when the tractor hit that second land mine. Didn't realise it, probably thought he had just bruised himself. Never stood a chance without immediate surgery.'

The man stood and walked to the lieutenant. He was nursing the hand wounded by Knifer's blade. His eyes widened when Knifer picked it up from the ground. Sam thought he was about to stab him, and was about to look away when she saw Knifer grab the man by the collar and deliver three sharp punches into Taylor's face before letting him slump to the ground.

'Sorry, needed to get that out of my system,' he said to the rest of the soldiers. Smicker had dismounted from his stolen vehicle and handed Knifer the bottle of whiskey.

'Get some of that into your system. You must be Knifer. I'm Smicker. Anyone else you want to hit a dig in the face?'

Knifer stared at the man in front of him who was as usual grinning. Smicker lit anther cigarette.

'Ahhh, back in the day I knew a few people who would have loved to work with you, you'd have made a fortune.'

Knifer drew deep from the bottle and said to Smicker, 'yeah I think I killed some of them.'

For one Smicker shut up and the grin slid from his face. Knifer laughed handed the bottle back and plucked the cigarette from Smicker's mouth and stuck it in his own.

'Fucker' was all that Smicker said, but he was grinning again.

Carragher walked over. 'I thought I recognised you. Loads of potential over the Brecons, then RTU, from there FRU'.

Before Knifer could reply, Sam interjected. 'Okay boys, you can wank each other off later, but we move out now.

CHAPTER 25

Jenny heard the perimeter before she saw it, the noise of the engines was drowned out by barking dogs. As they turned the final corner, they saw three large German Shepherds and two Rottweilers straining at leashes, each held by a single man. Flanking them were two women armed with rifles. Incongruously in front was a large, bearded man in a kilt holding a sword.

She waited as Seamus confirmed who they were. When they were asked for the password, he sighed and gave the one Smicker had agreed with them: Fuckers.

They moved slowly until level with the kilt wearer. He looked at the two soldiers in the door well, but Jenny spoke over them.

'Picked up some passengers along the way, don't worry they seem harmless enough for now.'

The sentry replied: 'Okay, everyone dismount. Walk past the dogs slowly.'

One by one they filed past the dogs. They looked ferocious, but instead they merely sniffed everyone as they walked by. The kilted man introduced himself to Jenny as Hamish and explained that the Icelandic vessels had picked them up from Scotland 10 days earlier.

Jenny walked through to what was the harbour area. Three trawlers, and several smaller boats were tied up. A larger boat was anchored a short way off. She could see the frigate near Rathlin.

One of the women holding a rifle walked over to Jenny, and said her name was Lilja.

'You must be exhausted, but we have little time,' she said. 'We will get the children boarded on the small boats and take them to the Baldur. Adults will go on the trawlers. All weapons are to be stored in the hold. They will be returned once the quarantine period has ended.'

Lilja's precise wording told her that the woman was reciting a script, but she was making the effort to sound pleasant, given English was not her first language.

'Are you the leader of this group?'

'Yes, but Sam and Greg in the other convoy are the real leaders.'

'When they arrive, we will meet with Bjorn and Inge, there is a delicate issue they will need to discuss with you all.'

Jenny was intrigued but she reached into her rucksack and handed Lilja a bottle of Bushmills whiskey.

'Oh, by the way the other group may arrive led by an armoured vehicle and a daft wee man who thinks everything is a joke.'

Chapter 26

Smicker was having a great time commanding the APC. Ordering the stoned driver to crash into random buildings, Firing the canon into the distance where he claimed 'there be dragons'.

However, Sam saw that what he was doing had more methodology, as several of the buildings contained the undead, and each pile of rubble left them trapped.

When they arrived at the Icelandic perimeter Smicker shouted the password and then moved the APC to form a barrier as the rest of the vehicles emptied and approached the guards and dogs.

'Who the fuck is yon man in the kilt,' he said. 'Is it fancy dress today?'

'Smicker, will you shut the fuck up for once in your life.'

Greg said he would take charge of the canon on the APC, in case anyone unwanted approached the perimeter. However, a shout from Jenny told him to leave it t someone else. After Elijah took up position he joined Sam in walking the last of the children and adults past the dogs and through into the harbour area.

Jenny ushered them to meet Lilja.

Greg, Sam? Would you please come with me.'

Sam gestured for Bryson to join them.

Walking to a hotel near the front they saw three Icelandic people and a small, huddled group of soldiers, watched over by Seamus.

A small woman came over and introduced herself.

'Hello. My name is Inge and we have a situation we need dealing with while we get everyone on board," she said. 'There are soldiers here who fired on the frigate, which is now under the control of the Icelandic government.

'They are saying they acted on the orders of the man there, a general he claims. He is not going to Iceland. But before we all go, we want to know what you plan to do with him.'

Knifer had joined them. He walked straight over to Brady.

'You know, I've just figured it out," he said to the general. 'I was wondering why there was so much ordinance about, why I'd been sent here to await orders. Why there are armoured personnel carriers, why there are so many special forces, and why you are trying to destroy that frigate.

'It was Plan Z. They probably didn't even tell you.'

He turned to the group. 'You see in the event of catastrophic collapse of government all naval submarines were to go to the River Foyle, that was assuming any were still afloat. There they would await orders and close the Iceland gap to Russian subs by any means necessary. The frigate could have detected submarines, even the stealthy ones.

'Fucking military doesn't know their history. That's where the Germans surrendered most of their submarines at the end of the last war. Everyone one of them was sunk there.'

Sam saw from Brady's expression he knew nothing of this plan.

She walked close to the man.

'Inspector Bryson, I believe, from what I have heard, constitute significant alleged crimes against multiple people. I think he should be detained. Can this be done?'

'If the police station is still standing, then he could be put in a holding cell awaiting formal charges. We have enough officers staying to do that.'

Sam turned to Brady, glanced at Greg, Knifer, Seamus, Carragher, and Smicker. They all nodded.

Inge, Lilja, would this be acceptable to you. They also nodded, but Sam thought that they would have preferred summary judgement and execution.

'We, general, on the authority of the people here, are charging you with crimes against the population of Northern Ireland. You know your limited rights, which I'm sure you will have formally read out to you.'

Brady straightened and lit a cigarette. He put the lighter in the deepest pocket of his trousers, and, pulled out a small pistol.

He brandished it around.

'If you think that I'm going to be put in a cell by some tinpot dictator, some treacherous soldiers and wannabe Vikings then you are wrong.'

Some of Lieutenant Taylor's men edged closer to Brady. Allen walked a few paces towards the general.

'Look sir, why don't you just hand that over to me and maybe negotiate with these people,'

He reached for the pistol. Brady shot the sergeant in the face before going to turn the gun on himself. Knifer's blade and Carragher's shot stopped his arm and Brady fell back, the gun dropping. His arm bleeding and the hole in his shirt where the bullet hit body armour.

'Ach fer fuck sake,' was Smicker's reaction as he reached Allen's body, looking at the mangled skull. Taylor looked anxiously on.

'Right, any loyal to that,' Sam said pointing at Brady, get out of here now. Go! Don't even think about returning. If any of you want to help keep any remaining people safe, speak to Greg, otherwise fuck off, fuck right off now.'

Seamus knelt over Brady. The general was bleeding profusely from where Knifer's blade had hit it. Brady was barely breathing. Pulling aside the shirt he saw the impact site of Carragher's bullet. The round had been dead centre on the heart. The impact would have caused catastrophic crushing of the ribs.

'Major," said Brady. 'I'll see you in hell.'

He died.

Chapter 27

Sam sat on the harbour wall. A bottle of whiskey in her hand and a joint in her lips. Greg walked over to her.

'Nearly time for you to be off,' he said.

'Yeah, the Icelanders want me and Jenny to join them on frigate. Most of the children are leaving now on the trawlers and that other boat. Rest should be on board in the next 15 minutes. I've told Smicker and

Seamus not to let Julie board, and now I'm telling you.'

'Why?'

'Wee Ruth died. Julie said I killed her, when it was that arse wipe Rambo. Ruth died saving children. Tried to tell her that but he slapped me, screaming at me. If Paul hadn't grabbed her, I would have let her keep on slapping. Did she not realise how fucked up I feel?

'She is a shit stirrer, and I don't want anywhere near what little sanctuary there is on a fucking island.'

Greg sat down beside her. He reached around her shoulders. Resting her head on his arm Sam began to sob.

'I don't know what I'm doing Greg. I don't know how to do anything, I've killed, I have watched others die horribly, I've…' Her voice tailored off.

'Listen, you know you are going to feel horrible.' Greg said. Whether it is in Iceland, or when you get back here. And that won't help,' he said pointing to the bottle. 'Whether you like it or not these people look up to you, they respect you, and they know you make big decisions when you need to.'

She stood, hugging Greg's lanky frame. She called Smicker, Seamus and Jenny over, hugging each in turn. They were the group who had started this journey with her, and had kept her sane.

'Good luck,' said Seamus.

'See you in Iceland,' said Jenny.

'Go on you mad wee cunt, take over that island and send us some pickled herring,' Smicker said as tears began trickle down his cheeks.

Greg shook her hand. 'Off you go then.'

Two of the soldiers from the group they encountered at the battle with the KKK and the zombies flanked her as she walked away. One, the Scouse driver, handed her the joint she had dropped. They appeared to have assumed position as her personal bodyguard.

She reached behind her, picked up the bottle of whiskey, raised it in the air and sad.

'Here's to you all. Sort this country out, stay sober Smicker, Seamus slap him every day, and Greg, take no shit.'

She turned, head down, and walked to the dinghy, ready to start her new life.

Epilogue

Standing on the edge of a rocky outcrop, three days after arriving in Iceland Sam was still processing the news. The call from Smicker, his voice straight and sober telling her Greg was dead.

A heart attack during a fight with zombies on the edge of Ballycastle. He told her they'd appointed Bryson to lead them.

'Middle name's Samantha, so we need one Sam here.'

The Icelandic government had welcomed her, put her in an office and asked her to take care of settlement of the new arrivals, and help make sure the coastal defences were being prepared. She was about to delegate that when the news came through as she was sitting in her office when the call came through.

Numb. That was all she felt. And alone.

She heard a faint cough behind her. Knifer.

'Sorry, that was shit news to hear,' he said. 'But I didn't know Greg well but I'm pretty sure he would have wanted you to carry on.'

She nodded.

'Anyway, before you get down to work, we're going to see a volcano.'

AUTHOR'S NOTE

Thank you for reading this book, and I hope you enjoyed it, or just even helped pass a few hours.

I hope you enjoyed the character's journey.

All geographical, military jargon and other details are liable not to be 100% accurate, despite research and advice. All errors are mine. Some might be deliberate.

I would be deeply grateful if you would post a review on Amazon or anywhere else, good or bad.

- Jonathan Traynor

ABOUT THE AUTHOR

Jonathan Traynor is a 58-year-old media professional, whose career in writing began when he graduated from Queens University, Belfast.

He has worked in newspapers and public relations, and was a key part of a multiple award-winning team with the Northern Ireland Commissioner for Children and Young People.

Race the Undead is Jonathan's third published book.